The Honeymoon Corruption

The Honeymoon Corruption

By Richard Lee Zuras

ISBN: 978-1-9399303-9-2

Library of Congress Control Number: 2015934112

Printed in the United States

Published by

Brandylane

In loving memory of my parents

Acknowledgements

I want to express heartfelt gratitude to my wife Kelly for the honesty she brings. Having my best friend as my first reader is an asset I do not take for granted. (Whether my endings work or not I judge from her countenance.)

I want to also thank Ray Rice and the entire faculty, administration, and staff at UMPI for their ongoing support. Also, I thank Robert Pruett and his wonderful staff at Brandylane, most especially my brilliant editor Erin Harpst. Together, we have all made this novel.

Finally I thank my extended family for their kind words. And to my sons, Everett and Holden, I write always with the hope that you will enjoy these books when you are older.

Althea Gearheart wore her wedding dress as she traversed the Wildwood boardwalk to the entrance of the Little White Wedding Chapel. She was already late to meet her fiancé, Guy Messersmith, and the early Memorial Day parade crowd wasn't making things easy for her.

The purpose of the meeting was to stage a quick rehearsal. Althea and Guy were eloping, and the dress was the only fine piece of clothing she had managed to pack. It was scarcely more than Easter garb, but she had received many compliments on it, and besides, Guy had proposed the elopement as the dress lay inanimate next to his bed.

Guy would not be angry at her tardiness, Althea reasoned, because he knew there was no one who could help Althea put up and style her long, blonde hair. Guy had offered, of course. She had said no, and Guy had instead gone off to secure the necessary paperwork for the marriage license.

Althea's shoes echoed on the boardwalk planks. Althea felt as though the Memorial Day crowd was staring at her, and she tried to make herself small. There she was, in full regalia, with an improvised veil pinned to her hair, strolling across the promenade in a kind of one-woman parade.

When she was a kid, Althea remembered, everyone had called the holiday Decoration Day, and she preferred to think of it that way. And now she was twenty years old, two days away from her marriage, and she did not want to think about all those Memorial Day dead, or about the headlines Guy had read to her, in the morning papers, describing the horrors of martial law in Montgomery, Alabama. It struck her that these opposite words *marital* and *martial* were spelled so similarly, and that here she was marrying in the sun, at a beach resort, while the Freedom

Riders, people her age, weren't even able to cross the state of Mississippi.

Guy was waiting for her outside the entrance to the Little White Wedding Chapel. He held a single pink carnation that seemed a bit unwilling to bloom fully, and he met her with the wide smile of a man who has been separated from his love for some time.

They kissed under the awning of the chapel.

"This is for you," he said.

Althea adjusted her veil and brushed her hair from her eyes. She buried her nose into the nape of his neck. He smelled like the carnation he held, as if he had transported it affixed behind his ear.

"I'm nervous and everyone is staring at me," she said.

"Relax," he said. "This isn't even real."

Althea pulled her head back and stared at Guy. She held on the subtle green freckles that peppered his brown eyes.

"Of course it's real," she said. She winked at him.

"It is kind of almost official though," Guy said. "I've got all the paperwork running through."

They stood and held hands. A seagull cooed from atop the chapel's makeshift steeple before clumsily chopping at the air with its wings as it dropped and brushed by the awning. Althea turned and watched the bird as it swooped here and there through the open air of the Wildwood boardwalk. The parade crowd had grown restless, and an old man reading the paper took a swing at the bird and missed, sending his newspaper flying over the railing and onto the beach.

Guy let out a laugh and studied the crowd.

"At least we're not the only ones dressed up," he said.

The sun flared from behind the clouds, and those respectful enough to have dressed for the parade took notice and stripped off their outer layers. Guy had, of course, dressed for a happier occasion than the mourners, but his flannel suit jacket left him just as uncomfortable. It was the only good jacket he owned, a gift from his uncle the day he admitted the elopement. When he left the farm in central Virginia, he had mistakenly assumed it would be much cooler in New Jersey. The suit smelled a bit like mothballs, but its thick material was soft and welcoming to Althea, and she clutched at it and rubbed Guy's arm anxiously. Guy placed the carnation under her nose.

"This smells better than my suit, I bet."

They took turns taking in the sweet fragrance and watched as the crowd began to settle, like lemmings, crammed against the boardwalk's side railings as the parade approached.

The chapel's small door opened behind them, and a man not nearly as tall as Guy appeared. He stood there for a moment, and then cleared his throat. Althea jumped a bit at this, and her veil pins caught on the generous fabric of Guy's suit, spilling her hair in uneven cascades across the bare skin of her shoulders.

"Sorry," the man said as he raised his hand like a traffic cop. "Startled you. So sorry."

"That's okay," Guy said. The men attempted to help Althea with her hair and veil.

"Oh. Oh, no," she said. She placed her hand up to shield her face. "I'll need a mirror."

"Of course," the man said.

Guy turned to look at the man, and found his eye drawn to his black collar.

"You are Pastor Kleiss?"

"Call me Neil."

"I'm Guy. This is my fiancée, Althea."

"Pleasure." The three nodded hurriedly at one another as they made their way through the small chapel, toward its changing area. "There is a mirror on the back wall."

Neil returned to the front door and shut it tightly. He watched Althea find her way into the changing room, then took Guy soundly by the arm and sat him down in a folding chair. He pulled up another and settled in.

"You two are in love?"

"We are."

"Nobody ever says no, but I ask." Neil rolled his thumb in his fingers. "You have absolutely no family or friends attending?"

Guy's voice grew sullen. "No."

Neil folded his arms, waiting for Guy.

"We ran away."

"From?"

"No. I mean, we are eloping. We're from a different state."

"Oh. For good reason or bad?"

"Father?"

"I am not a priest, my boy. I told you that when you called me. I am a pastor."

"I know. Habit."

"You are a Catholic?"

"I was raised up one." Neil reached out and touched Guy's shoulder.

"I have no issue with the Catholics, my boy. I even voted for John Kennedy and I'll do it again when his term is up."

Guy shifted on the hard chair. He turned toward the changing room.

"Althea. You okay in there?"

Althea opened the door a crack and nodded. She closed the door.

After a few minutes, the large grandfather clock chimed, and Neil pulled his chair around so that his back faced the changing room.

"I don't have an issue with elopers either, my boy. I don't mind Catholics and I don't mind doing this full dress rehearsal." Neil sat up straight and tall to meet Guy's eyes. "What I *do mind* is people getting married for the wrong reasons."

"I don't know what that means," Guy said. He now felt uncomfortable, and scooted his chair back. He hadn't liked to be talked to like that, not by anyone, since his parents passed away.

Neil stood up. He smiled.

"What I don't like, why I asked you if this is a wedding for good or bad reasons, is that I don't care to preside over *forced* weddings."

Guy shook his head. Neil dropped his hands to his belly. He brought his hands up, in a half-circle, from his waist to his chest.

"No," Guy said.

"Okay," Neil said. "Also, not every couple is fit to be married without some religious counseling."

Guy stood up, his thin frame looking even taller in the small room.

"Do you and your fiancée need to set up counseling?"

"If we could, Pastor, let's just get this over with."

The door to the dressing room opened the moment the words left his mouth. Guy did not need to see Althea's face to know how the words were received. Althea looked at him. He would not meet her eyes.

"Here I am," she said. And then she said, "Here we are."

She bumped him half on purpose as she made her way to the center of the small room. Given the half-length mirror and the dim light of the dressing room, she had fixed her hair and veil as best she could.

"I'm ready," she said.

Guy took his place next to her like a schoolboy. He kept silent, except for saying his lines in the ceremony.

After the rehearsal, the couple exited into a day that had become summer-like. Guy took Althea's hand and led her to the top of the stairs that led to the beach below.

"I shouldn't," she said.

"Your dress?"

She nodded. "My dress."

"Let's go and eat," he said. He locked his fingers in hers, and they walked the boardwalk.

"The parade crowd," he said. "It'll take us an hour to get anywhere."

Althea looked around. "Over there."

"Mack's Pizza," he said. "You sure?"

They crossed the crowded promenade and went in. The restaurant had a few booths and a counter. Behind the counter, two men stood, making pies as big as wagon wheels. The couple watched with wonder as the men pulled and stretched the dough, and flung the pies into the air again and again. When the pies were ready, the men slapped them down and ladled the centers with sauce before making looping circles, like a child's wondergraph.

"Smells like heaven," Althea said. One of the men pulled a half-pie out of the oven with a spatula the size of a snow shovel.

"Look," Guy said. "The sauce is so heavy, it mixes in with the cheese."

They took a seat at a booth, and Guy caught one man's attention and held up two fingers. The man nodded, and pulled two hot slices from the half-pie. He came over to the booth and set down the two slices and two small cups of water. Althea noticed that he stared at the top of her head.

"My veil," she said.

The couple freed the pins and secured the veil under the salt shaker.

"I look silly," she said.

They ate their slices in silence, Althea using her entire being to keep from dropping pizza sauce on her wedding dress. Guy finished and wiped his mouth. He offered Althea his extra napkin.

"I can't believe we have to wait two more days," Althea said. She pushed her remaining crust toward him. "So far, so good." She pointed at her dress. "Wasn't the greatest idea I ever had, though."

Guy smiled and finished her crust. He paid, and the couple returned to the boardwalk. The parade crowd had finally dispersed, and the people had scattered along the beachfront.

"Let's call someone," Althea said.

Guy looked at her. She could see his face lengthen.

"But people *will* want to know," she said.

"Know what?"

Guy reached for her hand, but she skipped ahead. She stopped and turned to face him, making a bullhorn with her hands.

"That we've eloped," she yelled.

A few people on the boardwalk smiled at Guy as they walked past. He stood there, waiting for her to come back. She walked halfway to him and stopped.

"The point of eloping," he said, "is that people *don't* know."

"I know," she said, "but it's like it hasn't happened if we don't tell people."

"It hasn't happened." He walked forward to meet her. "Yet."

She took his arm, and they walked along.

"But it will happen. It *is* happening, Guy. Don't you want to at least tell your uncle where we ended up?"

"Not really. The less he knows, the less your father can find out."

She pulled her body against his. For a minute or two, they stayed silent, and walked. The boardwalk was more crowded now, as they neared the amusement piers. The workers were out in force, even on this holiday, and they were hurrying to ready the rides before the adults had a chance to think about leaving. The roller coaster was the big attraction, and children tugged at their parents' arms in an effort to reach its growing line.

A woman in gypsy clothing beckoned Althea to come inside her alcove for a palm reading. An older man in the storefront next to the gypsy harassed Guy for not stepping up to test his strength and win a prize for his girl.

They walked down away from the long pier, and before they knew it they were cued up for the Tunnel of Love boat ride. A short teenage boy with a thick local accent asked Guy if the mister and missus wanted a free ride.

"I need to time the ride," he said. "See if my current is running too strong."

"Sure," Althea said.

She put her hands on Guy's back and shoved him toward the boat.

"Okay, okay," he said. "No need to shove me."

The teenage boy gave them a hand in getting on board. He stared at Althea.

"Pretty parade dress."

"Thank you," she said.

He gave the boat a shove with his foot and it rocked and eased its way toward the first tunnel. Althea turned and faced the boy.

"It's my *wedding* day," she yelled.

Guy craned his neck upward as the boat floated into darkness. "Did you see that?" he said. "The sign from the previous ride said it was called 'Ye Olde Mill.'"

"That's not so very romantic," she said. Then she kissed him on the mouth, missing somewhat at first, there in the dark, but finding it nonetheless. She pulled herself almost onto his lap before he broke the kiss.

"Your dress! It'll get wrinkled up, and we have no iron."

Althea wiped the lipstick from around his mouth with her finger as they moved into the sunlight between tunnels.

"I can just wash it and hang it," she said. "We have two whole days before the wedding."

Another boat bumped their boat from behind, and Guy was relieved to see that the trailing boat was empty. They watched empty boats line up in the space between the tunnels. From that point on, at every turn, darkness or light, the empty boats and their boat piled and bumped up on one another. Althea sat up straight, and smoothed her dress.

It wasn't until Althea and Guy neared their motel that Althea realized she'd forgotten her veil.

"It's lost," Guy said.

"No," Althea said. "We have to find it. I made it from the bow of my prom dress. Remember the bow?"

Guy shrugged.

"How can you not remember something from two years ago?"

"So we'll look for it," he said.

The couple turned and stared back in the direction of the boardwalk. Neither moved.

"Listen," Guy said, "I'll go and look for it and you can go back to the room."

Althea shook her head.

"Then why don't we walk to the beach, and I'll get on the boardwalk and look for your veil, and you can sit and watch the waves?"

Guy took her hand, and together they walked down Crocus Road to the sand dune entrance of the five-mile beach. No one was around to rent out a sun chair or umbrella, so Althea decided to go up onto the boardwalk with Guy. The five-block walk to the boardwalk's Wildwood Crest entrance was noisy, with people making their way back to the west side's wonderland of motels: the Ala Kai, the Coliseum, the Tempo, and the Crown Motel.

The couple had almost made it to their own motel, and now there they were, hot, tired, and walking the boardwalk again, unsure of where Althea had left her veil.

"Let's sit on this bench," Althea said. She sat down and stretched her arms toward the water. The Wildwood beach was wide, and when the tide went out the ocean receded like a far-off, beckoning oasis. "Maybe we should just forget about finding the veil."

"You're just saying that," Guy said. "It's okay. I'll find it."

"We're all the way at the edge of the boardwalk," she said. "It will take you forever."

Guy took off his suit jacket and placed it over the bench. Althea watched him as he slowly walked on, finally disappearing into the distant, growing crowd.

It had been more than an hour since Guy had left. Althea had dislodged her tight shoes and done all she could to keep her mind occupied. But the heat seemed to be waxing, and she felt perspiration overcome her dress.

She was thankful she had not worn a full slip. A couple came and posed their children along the railing for pictures, the ocean in the background. She thought about how Guy had forgotten to secure a camera, and that they would likely have no photos of their upcoming ceremony.

It began to bother her that Guy had left her alone on a bench for so long. She decided to go and wait under the boardwalk to avoid the sun. On the way down the stairs she lost her grip on her shoes, and then, Guy's coat. She watched as the coat caught the breeze and made a parachute that fell softly and obscured her shoes.

As she bent to retrieve the fallen items, a woman a little older than herself appeared out of nowhere. She had a large, friendly smile, and even somewhat short of breath from running, hands now atop her head, she seemed poised to help.

"Not too often," the woman said, "that one stumbles upon a young girl, in a swanky dress, carrying a man's woolen suit coat on a beachfront."

Althea blushed at this, and stumbled trying to right herself in the thick sand.

"Sand's a bit hot," the woman said. "Let me help you with all this." Then she said, "My name's Jeannie. Jeannie Ciminy, like Jiminy, as in Cricket."

Before Althea could respond, Jeannie had taken up Guy's coat and shaken the sand off of it. She held Althea's hand as Althea picked up her shoes. "I would say 'Cat's got your tongue,' but I've lived here forever and I've never seen a cat on this beach."

Althea smiled. She still had a grip on the woman's hand, and she gave it a light shake.

"I'm Althea Messersmith—I mean, Gearheart."

Jeannie pulled back her hand. "You mean you honestly don't know your own last name?"

"I do, I do." Althea looked around and absentmindedly straightened her dress. "I just got married. I mean I just *practiced* getting married."

"I don't think there's any practice for getting married, except . . . you know what I mean."

Althea started to sit on the last step, but Jeannie stopped her. "Don't sit there. These lowest steps always get mossy." She took Althea by the shoulder. "Why don't we get out of this sun? You look kinda pink."

"Okay," Althea said. It dawned on her that she had been heading under the boardwalk in the first place, and she followed Jeannie's lead.

Jeannie pulled out a pack of cigarettes and offered one to Althea.

"No, thanks. I don't smoke."

"Me neither," Jeannie said. "Not really." She put the cigarettes in her pants pocket. She had to work a bit to get them stowed.

"I'm holding these for Max. Do you know Max?"

Althea shook her head.

"Really? God. I thought everyone knew Max."

Althea shrugged.

"Max Castaldi?"

"Sorry."

Althea wrapped her arms across her chest. With only stray slices of sunlight cutting through the boardwalk planks, and with the deep cool sand giving away below, she felt a chill.

"I'm holding this," Jeannie said, extending the coat, "and here you are, in the shade!"

She walked behind Althea and wrapped the coat around her. "That will warm you right up. That coat has a nice, heavy gauge to it."

"It's my fiancé's," Althea said.

Jeannie put her hands up to her cheeks. "So you really are getting married?"

Althea smiled.

"When's the big day?"

"Thursday," Althea said. "Day after tomorrow. Actually, I shouldn't be standing down here out of sight for so long. Guy will be looking for me up on the boardwalk."

They made their way up the stairs. Halfway up, a young man passed them while attempting to slide down the railing. He fell off and just missed bowling them over. Althea looked back at Jeannie, who was grinning and shaking her finger at him.

"*Now*, Althea, you unfortunately know one—Mister—Max—Castaldi."

"Bet we've already met, baby."

Jeannie turned Max around and pushed him up the stairs past Althea. "Don't be such an *actor*."

Max twisted round to face the two women and awkwardly ascended the stairs. His hair reminded Althea of James Dean's; the cut was obvious, and he completed the look with a white T-shirt and black leather jacket.

"Jeannie, baby, you got my due backs?"

Jeannie wrestled the pack of Lucky Strikes from her pocket and handed them to Max. "I lost your matches," she said.

Max walked ahead of them on the boardwalk and patted at his jacket. He produced a flashy silver Zippo. He flared the lighter, then capped and returned it, along with the pack of cigarettes, to his inside jacket pocket.

"Max," Jeannie said as she deposited herself on a bench, "this is my new friend, Althea."

"New? You guys look tight to me."

"She's one of the good ones," Jeannie said. "And she's getting married, so keep your greaser hands off her."

Max pulled his lighter back out and retrieved a Lucky from behind his ear. "The apple butter will get you nowhere."

Jeannie draped her arm around Althea. "Don't worry about him, Althea; he's a real cat but he don't really bite."

Althea smiled. A part of her delighted in having some other people around. But she knew the day was getting away from her, and she wondered if she should go back to the Satellite Motel to look for Guy. She was certain they had missed each other.

"Max is actually a good person to know. In spite of his personality," Jeannie said. "I've known him since we were in diapers."

"Since we were a couple of ankle-biters," Max said. "Yep. That's the truth." He stubbed out his cigarette and offered his jacket to Jeannie. She shook her head.

"Getting married," he said. "I probably know the guy."

Jeannie giggled. "Sorry," she said, nudging Althea. "You probably get that all the time." Althea nodded, and forced a laugh.

"What's the big tickle?" Max asked.

"Her fiancé's *actual* name is Guy."

"Oh," he said. "I used to know a guy named Guy. French guy from Quebec City."

"No," Althea said. "He's Irish. I mean, probably more Irish than anything else."

Max laughed. "He's a mutt then. That's cool."

Althea nodded. "I think he has some Welsh and a bunch of other things."

Max laughed again. Then he made some barking noises.

"Max," Jeannie said, "you are such an *Iti*."

"So are you," he said. "I just show mine off."

Jeannie shook her head at him. "I'm an American. And so are you, Max. We were born in America and so were all four of our parents."

"So?"

"So? So stop acting like you're so hip to Italy all of a sudden and go back to just being the greaser we all know and love."

Max laughed and pulled out his pack of cigarettes. He offered one to Althea.

"She doesn't smoke," Jeannie said.

Max returned the cigarettes to his jacket. "I've been to *Little* Italy several times, you know."

The three of them laughed together. Max sat down on the bench next to Jeannie and nudged them over with his hips. They sat there for a few minutes, watching people. Occasionally, a tandem bicycle would go by, careful to keep its tires running smoothly along one of the boardwalk's two cement paths.

When Guy spotted Althea, at first he didn't think it was her. He had brought her to Wildwood, New Jersey for two reasons: the ocean, and the fact that they knew not a single soul.

Althea recognized Guy immediately, and waved to him. Guy held his hand aloft and waved her veil. He could see her smiling from where he was, and he dodged the occasional bike as he strode slowly to her side.

Max met him first, hand extended. "Max Castaldi."

Guy took Max's hand and shook it. He kept his eyes, though, on Althea. "Guy Messersmith."

Althea got up and came over to Guy. "You actually found it," she said. Guy handed the veil to Althea.

"Your lady lost her crown, eh?" Max said. "Ain't that a bite?"

Guy turned to Max. "What's that?"

"Nothing," Max said. "Take a load off."

The four of them attempted to wedge themselves onto the bench. The fit was too tight.

“I’ve an idea,” Jeannie said. “Let’s all go and have a drink and get to know one another.”

“We’re only twenty,” Guy said. “Althea just turned it, in fact.” Althea nodded. “And we should probably get going.”

“Call me, then,” Jeannie said as she and Max got up to leave. Althea started to say something, and Jeannie grabbed her hand and wrote her phone number on Althea’s palm. “We girls gotta stick together, Althea.”

And with that, Jeannie and Max descended to the beach.

When Guy and Althea arrived back at the Satellite Motel, it was near dinnertime.

“I wonder,” Althea said, “should I call Jeannie and say thanks for keeping me company?”

“Your dime,” he said.

“Our dime,” she said.

Guy broke away from her and took the stairs to the Satellite’s raised patio two at a time. He stood there, outside the motel’s lobby, and stationed himself to look down at the pool. He could tell from looking down on the parking lot that most of the tenants had checked out that morning. It was the first time since their Saturday arrival that he had seen the pool and parking lot so empty. Althea followed Guy’s pensive stare, and turned to look at the pool from outside its little fence.

Above Guy’s head, the motel’s blue-and-white neon sign buzzed on. It would be a while before its neon glow could fully rain down on the pool below. For now, the motel’s unique triangular windows sparkled, reflecting the setting sun. Guy turned and pressed his face to the lobby window. Inside, a middle-aged woman in a robe sat behind the counter. She flipped through a book, and occasionally wrote in it.

Althea climbed the stairs. As she passed Guy, she thought he might follow her, and so she waved him toward the pool.

Althea looked down at her palm. She had sweated during their walk, but not enough to obscure the numbers. She neared the woman in the robe and wished for a moment that she and Guy had a working phone in their own room.

The woman looked up from her book.

“I need to make a phone call.”

The woman picked up a sea-green phone and placed it on the counter. "Local?"

Althea nodded. She dialed the number and got no answer. She extended her fingers, stretched her palm out, and reread the number. She dialed again. After eight rings, she replaced the receiver.

"Could I ask you to write down a number for me and keep it here?"

The woman found a pencil and a scrap of paper. Althea read out the number and the woman wrote it down, then turned and placed it in a wooden cubby with the spare room keys.

Althea looked around, found the lobby's bathroom, and went in. She scrubbed her hand under lukewarm water. The numbers faded, but would not come off entirely.

Outside, she found that Guy had stripped to his shorts and entered the pool. Althea sat at the top of the stairs and watched him swim.

Hudson's was crowded, but the place was capable of handling the flow of the dinner rush. Althea and Guy found a booth near the back of the restaurant. The waitress came by and tried to drop off menus, but they quickly informed her they wanted two orders of meatloaf and potatoes, no veggies.

The waitress brought their food to them before they could even start a conversation. They ate hungrily without speaking. Halfway through the meal it occurred to Althea that she had been wearing her wedding dress all day. She thought, but did not say, that either they were already married, or this truly was not a wedding dress.

"Excuse me, Guy," she said.

She stood up and dotted the corners of her mouth with a napkin. After waiting for the young busboy to go by their table, she turned and walked to the back of the restaurant, and found the pay phone near the rest rooms. She placed the coins in the phone and opened her hand. She dialed the number mostly from memory, but needed to glance down at her hand for assistance.

A man answered.

"Yes, hello. I'm calling to see if Jeannie is available to talk?"

"Hey. That Althea? It's Max!"

"Yes. Hello."

The phone made a muffled sound for a second, and then she heard Max yell for Jeannie.

"Althea? Hey," Jeannie said. "How's the honeymoon?"

"We're not married yet."

"I know, I know. Listen, why don't you guys come over here and celebrate? You can drink here, you know."

Althea twirled the phone cord. "I don't know, Jeannie. I really just called to say thanks for, well, that it was nice meeting you. And Max."

Jeannie laughed. "Okay." Then she laughed again. "Stop doing that, Max."

The phone line clicked off.

Althea returned to the booth and sat opposite Guy. They finished their birch beers and Althea leaned in to get Guy's attention.

"I think I want Jeannie and Max to come to our wedding. You know, as witnesses."

The next morning the couple had nothing scheduled. It was the day before their wedding, and they had no plans to make or appointments to keep. They had assumed they would spend the day on the boardwalk and at the beach, but it was raining hard, and the day was looking like a total loss. They talked about watching the console television in the lobby, but instead, they stayed inside and watched the sheets of rain come in at sharp angles.

Around lunchtime, Guy decided to at least attempt a run to Hudson's. When he opened the door to leave, he found himself face to face with the motel manager. Althea looked over Guy's shoulder, and saw that the woman from the lobby was there with him.

"There's a woman named Jeannie," he said, "calling here for Althea. That's your wife, right?"

Althea rushed a hello and pulled her shoes on quickly. The manager and the woman walked back toward the lobby under a large umbrella. Guy handed Althea a newspaper, and she kept it over her as best she could as she followed them.

Inside the lobby, the manager handed her the phone and told her to make it fast. Althea nodded and took the receiver.

"Jeannie. Thanks for calling!"

"I remembered you said you were at the Satellite."

"Did I?"

"I guess. Max said he remembered."

Althea turned her back toward the manager. She had seen that he was listening to every word.

"So why don't you and Guy come out with us? We're heading to the movies."

"Really?"

"Sure. I think Max wants to see *Return to Peyton Place*."

Max and Jeannie arrived to pick them up in a blue-and-white Packard Hawk. The model was a couple years old, but Guy was impressed. It had a few scratches, but its fins were thick and long, and the grille, he thought, was mean and cool.

Max held the door open, and Guy and Althea got in the back and said hello to Jeannie, who sat up front. The car was dry and warm, and the interior was as clean and white as could be. Althea smiled at Guy, reached forward, and touched Jeannie on the shoulder. The three of them watched as Max, after slamming the door, feigned a jump across the hood. He stopped at its midpoint and ran his fingers slowly across the conspicuous, muscled bump of the Hawk.

"He's such an actor," Jeannie said. She said it, Althea thought, with equal parts annoyance and affection.

"You'll have to excuse Max. He thinks he's back in 1956, on his graduation day."

Max winced at Jeannie's insult, bumped up against Althea's window, and mooned them with his jeaned rear end. He got in and started the Hawk. It came on strong, and Max revved the engine a few times before he turned to face Althea.

"What do you think? Want to feel what this bent eight can do?"

Jeannie punched Max in the arm. "That's not funny, Max."

Max let out a laugh. "I'm just goofing around. Guy's a guy. He understands.

"But okay, seriously," he said, "no backseat bingo, you two." He waggled his finger as he said it, then turned and pulled the Hawk out of the parking lot.

It didn't take long to drive to the Strand Theater. Max didn't seem to use the brake if he didn't have to. The couple spent the ride bouncing off one another as if they were riding in a Hollywood stunt car. Occasionally, Max drove through a pool of water at the side of the road, and a plume of spray inked his window.

When he exited the car, Guy quickly slammed the door behind him. He settled under the marquee and stared at the posters for the coming attractions. Max escorted Althea and Jeannie to the ticket window. When the four of them teamed, Max led them to the balcony seats. The main feature was just beginning.

They emerged in a crowd of weekend employees who had come there to dodge the rain, and to fill their day. Max slung his arm around Jeannie and raised his voice for everyone to hear.

"That was one crappy movie!"

"Then why did you take us?" Jeannie asked.

"Because," Max said, "the first Peyton movie was—I saw it senior year. With you, maybe? It was cool. *And sexy*."

Jeannie pulled herself out from under his arm. "Max, I don't know why I spend my time with you."

Max stopped, pulled up his collar, and cocked his head slowly at Jeannie. "It wasn't with *you*?"

Jeannie looked up at the sky. "At least the rain has stopped."

"I could go for something sweet," Althea said.

"You guys haven't had Laura's fudge? It's the best," Max said.

Althea shook her head. Jeannie came over and took Althea's hand, and ran ahead with her. Guy and Max followed.

Laura's was not a large shop, but the smell of its sweet confections overwhelmed the block leading to its doors. The exiting traffic from the Strand Theater seemed almost to follow the foursome, and the shop soon filled with dozens of jostling people.

Max ordered a sampler platter, a pound of fudge in all, and the four of them used napkins to dry off the seats at an outdoor table. The boardwalk was only a block to the east, and they stationed their chairs next to one another so they could all face in its direction. Each of them took a piece of fudge and Althea and Jeannie made *oohing* sounds as they ate.

"Tell us about your wedding," Jeannie said.

Althea swallowed her piece of fudge and looked at Guy. He was silent. "It's not really a wedding," she said. "More of a ceremony."

"We're elopers," Guy said.

"Del Shannon!"

Althea and Guy both shrugged. Max put down the mint fudge he held. "Del Shannon? 'Runaway?'" Jeannie rolled her eyes at Max and scooted her chair closer to Althea. Max wound up and lightly punched Guy on the arm. "You do like rock and roll music, don't you, Guy?"

"I guess. Haven't heard much, really."

"I'm so excited for you," Jeannie said. "A wedding is a big step!"

Althea nodded. She noticed that Jeannie did not stop smiling.

"Can I see your dress?"

Althea looked at Guy.

"Listen to me. I'm being so forward," Jeannie said.

"No," Althea said. "You're fine." She took a piece of walnut fudge in her fingers, and then set it back down.

Jeannie pulled back, away from Althea. "No . . . Yesterday? That dress?"

Althea nodded. Max kicked at Jeannie from under the table.

Jeannie lifted her eyebrows. "Yes, yes. No, it's . . . lovely—I could help you with it!"

Max finished swallowing his fudge. "Jeannie's a regular seamstress. She can do practically anything with that Singer sewing machine of hers."

"We're fine," Guy said, standing up. "Thanks for the movie and the fudge. Really kind of you." He motioned for Althea to get up.

"I'm a fool," Jeannie said.

"Yeah, just ignore her," Max said. "Always trying to butt in."

Jeannie kicked at Max, but hit the stem of the table. A cup of water tipped, and some splashed onto the plate of fudge. Max scooped up the fudge and wiped at it with a napkin.

Guy took Althea by the elbow and nudged her to leave. As they said their good-byes, Max pointed in the direction of their motel and offered them a ride. Guy waved him off, and the couple started the thirty-block walk to the Satellite Motel.

By the time they reached their room, they were soaked from the lingering humidity. Althea passed out on the bed, her shoes dangling off the edge. Guy closed the drapes and went out and bought a *Philadelphia Daily News*. He started back to their room, but thinking of Althea sleeping inside, he sat down on the metal chair in front of their room and read.

The paper was full of stories about the crash of a DC-8 in Lisbon that had killed sixty-two people. Guy put the paper on his lap, and his mind wandered to the story he had recently read about Kennedy setting America's sights on the moon.

He heard a noise in the room, and peeked through the small crack where the drapes met the windowsill. It was dark, but he could make out Althea's shape on the bed. He figured the noise was simply Althea removing her shoes.

He took up his paper and read some more about the DC-8, then opened to the sports reports. He scanned the box scores, looking for word on his hometown team, the Washington Senators—but the embarrassing conversation from Laura's Fudge kept playing in his mind, as though it were on a loop.

That last evening of May came in cool and clear. Althea had slept most of the afternoon, and she was restless.

They decided to have their one planned, fancy dinner at Zaberer's Restaurant. They walked down Aster and onto the beach and asked a sun-tanning family if they knew where the restaurant was. "I saw it on a flying airplane ad," Guy said. "It's supposed to be some kind of fancy restaurant."

The father squinted north, into the distance. "I think it's near the amusement piers. Maybe down a ramp off the street-side of the boardwalk."

Guy thanked the man, and he and Althea walked up the beach, toward the amusement piers. The seagulls squawked for food, as if they had never eaten a proper meal in their lives. Althea shivered each time the sun found a building and left her. After a while, the sun's heat was absent, the effect coupling noticeably with the ocean breeze. Althea pulled Guy closer and led him up to the boardwalk. They still had blocks to go before they reached Zaberer's.

By the time they reached the placard that pointed the way, they were famished. They found a dinner menu affixed to Zaberer's window, and they stood and read it in its entirety. Althea said "You try this" and "We should get one of these" before she noticed Guy's expression.

Guy turned away from the menu and stood looking across the boardwalk to the sea.

"I wish I had a cigarette," he said.

Althea came to his side. She looked at his extended hand. It shook.

"And I don't even smoke," he said.

He walked onto the boardwalk. Althea followed.

"I had no idea it would be so expensive when I heard about the place."

"We don't have to eat here," she said. "There are lots of restaurants."

"The whole place," he said. "And we aren't working yet, so every day . . . It just adds up so fast."

"I know," she said. "That's why I haven't asked to go on the Hunt's Pier rides."

"Sorry," he said.

She reached up and kissed him on the cheek. "I could just get my father to send me money."

Guy took her hand, and they started walking toward North Wildwood. "He won't send it to you here. With me. You know that."

Althea sighed. "I know. Anyway, I'd get sick on the spinny rides."

A long yellow tramcar approached them from behind. A recording blared out its warning: "*Watch the tramcar, please.*"

Guy pulled Althea toward him, and they stood and watched the tram as it drove slowly by, car by connected car. It stopped, and the couple watched as people paid their fares and got on. As the last car passed, Althea saw Guy's face sadden.

"There was that fortune-teller," she said. "We should do that for fun one day. That should be cheap."

Guy gave her a little smile.

By the time they reached Young Avenue and the Wildwood Diner, they felt like the seagulls they had witnessed on the beach. They climbed the stairs into the lime green diner and took up a booth near the kitchen entrance. The place was loud with regulars—locals; older men and their wives out for a boardwalk shuffle and a good, solid meal in the middle of the work week.

Guy quickly decided on a hamburger and a shake, and Althea

ordered the same. They took turns using the rest room, and when their meals arrived, they ate them quickly. They paid the bill and moved along as the busy diner quickly filled their booth with hungry people from the boardwalk.

They were not used to such constant walking, especially coupled with the spare amount of food they had eaten. They took a minute to stretch and relax on a bench overlooking the ocean.

"I wish I had a car," Guy said. He opened his wallet, looked through it, and put it away.

When the Tramcar approached, heading south, they got on, and Guy reluctantly paid their fares. Each time the slow tram stopped to load and unload passengers, Guy mentioned that it was actually worse than walking.

"Still," Althea said, "I guess it's nice to go slow and just look around."

They passed a sign for the Packard Motel.

"We'd already be home," she said, "if we were staying at the Packard."

Guy looked at her, and then back at the ocean. "Funny you mention Packard of all things," he said, voice low.

"Maybe I wish you had a car, too," Althea said.

When they finished walking from the end of the Tramcar route to the Satellite Motel, they found the manager standing outside their room. He was larger than Guy had noticed before, and seemed to struggle as he attempted to balance and tie his shoe against the metal chair.

"I've got someone who's needing to rent this room," he said. He pulled his foot off the chair and slammed it down on the concrete.

Guy took out his key, looked down at the manager's still unlaced shoe, and attempted to bypass him.

The manager used his heft to block the couple's path. "Loved having you," he said, "but a deal's a deal."

"What does that mean?" Althea asked.

Guy reached out and gave Althea the room key.

"It means," the manager said, "this family that's coming in is paying full price. Weekend price, even." He politely stepped back so that Althea could enter the room.

"It's okay, Althea," Guy said. He took back the key from Althea and opened the door, then shut it quickly behind them.

"They were letting us have the room for six dollars a night. As long as they didn't need it," Guy said.

"And now they do?"

"I guess the season's picking up already."

Althea sat on the edge of the bed. Guy began to pack their clothes in two duffel bags.

Guy zipped up the first duffel bag, then sat down in a chair.

"I don't have that kind of in-season, weekend money," he said.

The manager knocked on the door. "Tomorrow," he said loudly.

"How do we check out *tomorrow*? Guy? And get *married*?"

Guy pulled the drape back and looked into the parking lot. He watched the manager limp off. "I figured we'd have more time before they needed the room."

Althea pulled off her shoes and crawled under the covers.

"It's too late to go looking for a place tonight," Guy said. "We'll do it tomorrow."

"I'm not getting married if I'm homeless."

Guy let go of the drape and sat still in the chair. "I know."

"My father might send *my* money," Althea said, "if I call and tell him I really need it."

Guy walked to the bathroom. He stood in the doorway.

"You know you can't call your father. And my uncle really can't help us. It's just us, now, Althea."

"I know," she said. "I know that."

It was nearly nine-thirty when they awoke. Guy filled two glasses with water from the sink, and they drank them and dressed. They packed their few remaining toiletries into the duffel bags and walked the long block to Hudson's restaurant, Guy shouldering the full load.

Inside, the restaurant was crowded and noisy, and the only open seats were two stools at the counter. They ordered the bacon and egg special and ate and watched their bags, which Guy had placed on the floor in the corner, under the hat rack. When they finished, it was nearing eleven—only three hours until their scheduled wedding at the Little White Wedding Chapel.

Althea went to the pay phone and tried to call Jeannie. She kept dialing incorrect phone numbers, the digits now mostly erased from her palm. Eventually, Guy ran out of change, and they left the restaurant.

Outside, the day was heating up, and they sat atop the duffel bags on the corner next to Hudson's. People filed in and out of the restaurant, occasionally pausing to look at the couple before going about their day. Behind them, a man worked on an anthropomorphic ice cream cone sign. Its painted azure eyes peered from behind bent neon. The ice cream cone's legs were crossed and ended in two baby blue shoes.

In the starkness of the morning sun, the sign looked sad, out of place. The man had taken it off the restaurant's façade. Free of its metal attachments, it looked to Althea as if it had been riddled with bullets from the pistol of a two-bit movie gangster.

"You don't remember Jeannie's number at all?"

Althea shook her head. "No. But we could get it from the office at the Satellite." Guy looked at her and tilted his head. "I had the woman at the desk keep it. She probably still has it."

Guy shook his head.

"They were nice people. I'm sure they wouldn't mind us calling Jeannie's number on the lobby phone."

Guy stood. He looked around, shielded his face from the sun with his hand.

"You're too proud to ask them for the number, aren't you? Because they put us out of our room."

Guy grabbed the duffel bag he had been sitting on. He placed it next to Althea. "I'll be right back," he said.

Althea watched Guy reenter the restaurant. Then she turned and watched the man working on the sign. She could tell he had been watching their spat.

"People call this fella 'cone man.'"

Althea smiled. She watched the worker wipe his brow with a bandana and hoist the cone man into his truck. He feigned a tip of his hat to her, and she nodded at him in return. She watched him drive his truck onto Atlantic Avenue, the cone man waving as they vanished into the distance.

She heard the door behind her open, and Guy emerged with a slip of paper raised high in his hands like a trophy.

"What's that?"

"It's Max's address." Guy handed the paper to Althea. She read it and handed it back. "Some people in there know this Max fella a little bit." Althea stood and grabbed one of the bags.

"It's about a half mile or so. Oh. And you won't believe this. Max lives on 'Forget Me Not Road,'" Guy said.

"I saw that road," Althea said.

She started walking, and Guy fell in with her. "When?"

"Last week. When we were checking into our motel." She held out her heavy bag to switch with his.

"Sorry," he said.

"We came down Pacific Avenue and I started seeing all these beautiful names on the cross streets. There was 'Forget Me Not' and 'Primrose' and 'Orchid.' Our motel was on 'Aster,' didn't you notice?"

"Notice what?"

"All flowers," she said.

It wasn't the long walk but the weighted bags that slowed their trek. At the intersection of Atlantic and Forget Me Not, Guy put down his bag and jogged alone up the western side to see which way the numbers ran. Before he made it to Sunset Lake, he caught sight of some house numbers and turned around. They walked down Forget Me Not, east toward the ocean, sure that they were going the right way.

Max's address was a split Victorian house with each apartment marked by a letter. Guy checked the slip of paper he had gotten from the restaurant.

"No apartment letter," he said.

They set down their bags, and Guy walked in a circle around the entire building. "I don't see his Hawk."

A voice called down, and the couple took a few steps back and looked up. On the top floor, about forty feet up, a woman leaned over a short balcony railing.

"Althea? Is that you?"

Althea waved. Jeannie was wearing next to nothing, and watering rooftop flower boxes.

"Come up," she said. She finished watering the flowers and leaned over the railing. "Top floor!"

Althea left Guy with the two bags and scampered into the building and up the stairs. Jeannie met her in the small hall outside the apartment. She hugged her.

"You're out of breath," Jeannie said. Althea nodded, and kissed her forcibly on the cheek.

"What's going on, Althea?"

Althea entered the apartment. She crossed the living room and sank into the love seat. Guy's distant voice startled her, but she stayed motionless as she watched Jeannie move out of the apartment and onto the stairs. For a minute, Althea was alone.

She rose, and without thinking, toured the small penthouse. She picked up items and put them down in the wrong places as she sidled along. Fabrics that caught her eye she stroked, and she haphazardly opened and closed cabinet doors.

Jeannie, followed by Guy, entered the apartment, and they watched Althea without being noticed.

"Max will be home soon," Jeannie said. "This is *his* place."

Althea finished her tour and slid back onto the love seat.

"Max will figure out something," Jeannie said. "Whatever you need." She put down the duffel bag and turned to Guy, and motioned for him to do the same. "Why don't you stretch out over here?"

The pair took Althea by the hands and moved her to the bed. "I just made it up fresh this morning. Go on. Take a rest," Jeannie said.

Jeannie went to the sink and filled a glass of water for Althea. She offered it to her and took a seat at the edge of the bed.

"Maybe some music," Jeannie said.

She crossed the room and disappeared behind a curtain. Guy heard the click of an electric device, and a scratching sound.

"This is the new Ricky Nelson record. Max just got it." Jeannie came out from behind the curtain and sang "Travelin' Man" along with the record. Althea sat up and watched as Jeannie crooned with Ricky about various lovers. She looked around and fantasized about the apartment, wishing it were big enough for four. The mattress was much firmer than the one at the Satellite, and it felt comfortable beneath her. Guy came over and kissed her on the forehead.

"Why don't you just take a rest?" he said.

Althea nodded. She made herself comfortable on the bed, and Guy removed her shoes. He walked across the room and placed them next to the bags, then motioned Jeannie over. They went into the hall and closed the door most of the way behind them.

"What happened?" Jeannie asked. She placed her hand on Guy's shoulder, and he lowered his head.

"We got the boot. Kicked out of our motel room."

"But it's your wedding day!" she said.

Guy backed against the wall and rubbed his knuckles into his dark crew cut.

"There's no wedding," he said.

Jeannie turned and closed the door. "Who told you that?"

"No one," he said. "It just feels . . . How can we get married? We have no place to live. My money went so quick."

"Listen," she said. She put a finger up to his lips. "Let's just wait for Max and he'll figure something out. Max knows practically everyone. I'm sure he can fix this."

Guy put his head in his hands.

"I don't know what I was thinking," he said.

When Max arrived, he found Guy outside the apartment, on the stairs.

"Got hot out there today," Max said.

Guy looked up and watched as Max placed his jacket on the stairs and sat on top of it. Then he fired up his Zippo and breathed in his cigarette.

"My own place, you know? And I'm not even allowed to smoke in it."

He laughed. He patted his pockets and extracted his car keys. "Let's agitate the gravel awhile. Yeah?"

Guy studied him. In the dim light he thought Max looked more like Ricky Nelson, rather than the James Dean he played. Either way, his hair was thick and with his way of dressing and speaking, he had a certain charm and strength.

Max got up and opened the door. He called to Jeannie that they were leaving, and shut the door before she could respond.

When they reached the Hawk, Guy saw that Max had put the top down. The day's sun had reached its apex. The time of the wedding had come and gone.

Max popped the Hawk's hood and invited Guy over with a subtle wave. The engine was freshly cleaned, he said, and he waved his hand carefully across the heat that rose from the Hawk's engine, as though he was absorbing its aura.

"That," Max said, "is a McCulloch Supercharger. Two-hundred and seventy-five horsepower." He pulled his hand back and stroked the fender. "She's a classy chassis, but that charger is what blows off the hot-rodders."

"It's a nice car," Guy said.

"Oh yeah, it is! I get cranked about it."

The more Guy listened to Max talk, the more he started to feel numb.

"Let's go," Max said.

He slammed the hood, ran around, and jumped over the driver's side door. Guy started to follow his lead, then stopped, opened the passenger door, and climbed in. The noises from the Hawk's engine reverberated off the building, and Max revved it for full effect.

They pulled out of the apartment's parking lot and headed south on Ocean Avenue. Max dialed the radio up and down, pausing here and there when he heard doo-wop or a familiar rock and roll song. They reached Farragut Avenue, and Max slid the Hawk into the parking lot of the Saratoga Motel.

"I guess, Max, that Althea called you?"

Max killed the ignition. "She caught me at work. I was about to head up to Atlantic City."

Guy looked at the floor.

"I have to run a quick errand," Max said. "I'll be back."

Max climbed over the seat and hopped off the top of his door. Guy watched as he went past the Saratoga and disappeared between motels.

Guy reached over and turned the key, and played with the radio dial. He put his arm across the top of the driver's seat, and turned and looked at the tuck-and-roll. He pictured himself riding in that backseat with Althea. Then he looked at Max's seat and pictured himself driving. Maybe to Atlantic City.

When Max came back into view, he grinned at Guy and pretended to sing along to the radio, into an invisible microphone. He bowed at Guy and laughed. "I still can't believe that Buddy Holly's dead."

Guy faked a smile. He didn't really know much about Buddy Holly.

Max got in and started up the Hawk. It wasn't long before he had them cruising north on Atlantic, into the heart of Wildwood. He swung the car into the lot of the Wildwood Diner. Max hopped out and again disappeared into a motel. Guy couldn't make out the name on its worn sign.

He got out of the Hawk and closed the door behind him. The sand dunes were visible from here, and the air smelled faintly of salt. He could read the sign on the motel across the street: the Stardust. It was the motel that inspired him to choose Wildwood for the elopement. His uncle was a Sinatra fan—Guy had heard practically every song—and Guy had read that Sinatra had hung out there, slept right *there* in the Stardust Motel. He wondered what his uncle might think.

He opened his wallet and counted what was left of his money. He gazed at the Stardust, picturing what it would be like to rent the suite Sinatra always used. He and Althea, in Sinatra's room.

He closed his wallet and waved back at Max, who was signaling to him from across the street. Max came over and climbed atop the back bumper. Then he hopped down and reached out.

"You'll want to shake my hand," he said.

Guy took it. They shook.

"Here's the deal," Max said. "I got you set up at the Skylark Motel. It's not *forever*, but I've got you covered for a while."

Guy looked back at the motel whose sign he couldn't quite read.

"How much?"

"How about you pay me three dollars a day to cover it, friend."

Max slapped Guy on the back and climbed into the Hawk.

Max's apartment would not have been so cramped had Althea not opened both duffel bags and removed their contents. Jeannie had strung a rope diagonally across the apartment, and the pair hung Althea's clothing indiscriminately. The pants and dresses and blouses formed a makeshift demarcation, dividing the apartment into unequal halves. Max and Guy resided in the smaller unit, having taken up quarters near the record player. Jeannie and Althea relaxed in the section that housed the bed.

Max churned through his record boxes, stopping here and there to switch the record. He played mostly Elvis, early hits, and some Eddie Cochran. Jeannie consoled Althea by plucking an article of Althea's clothing off the line and showing her how the factory could have made it prettier with a slight change in hue, how a stitch might have been stronger at a fault point, or how she and Althea could accentuate a curve through a simple variation in a hem line. She spoke to Althea of designers, labels, manufacturers Althea had never even heard of: French names; Italian names; names that were, according to Jeannie, only available stateside in Manhattan. They discussed the Chanel outfits Jackie Kennedy wore. Jeannie showed Althea the pillbox hat Max had bought her when he was last in New York.

When the record player went dead for a minute, Jeannie said, "Max, honey. Could you play us that Shirelles record? You know the song I like."

Max sighed audibly, as Jeannie smiled at Althea. He placed the record on the turntable and dropped the stylus on "Will You Still Love Me Tomorrow." Jeannie hummed along with the record, reached up, and removed the simple bag that held Althea's wedding dress.

"Not to be rude, Althea, but this is more of a Sunday dress. Isn't it?"

Althea lowered her head.

"That was rude of me," Jeannie said. She lifted the dress up out of the bag and turned it.

"I know. Althea. Listen to this idea: we could make you a dress."

"I can't ask you to do that."

The song stopped.

"Max! You could have played the whole *album*, you know."

They heard Max force a laugh. Guy crawled under the clothing divider and joined them.

"What are you two doing?"

Max cued the needle on the next song. There was a pop, and then a doo-wop version of "Blue Moon" played.

Althea placed her hand on Guy's. "Jeannie and I are—" She looked at Jeannie. "—thinking of making a real wedding dress." She lifted her chin and smiled at Guy.

"And I have an idea," Jeannie said. "Why doesn't Althea stay here, and we can get started?"

Guy turned and looked at the clock. He already knew it was getting late. He thought about the dresses Althea had at home—the ones her father had taken from her closet and burned.

"Yes," he said. "That's a good idea."

Max drove Guy to the Skylark. Guy stood outside his new room, holding the bag he had packed with his things, and watched Max drive away. It was past dinnertime, and Althea had sworn she'd be along at a reasonable hour. He put his bag in the room and decided to walk down Spicer to the boardwalk.

It was a hot summer night, and the weekend crowd had already arrived. It wasn't like the weekend before, when he and Althea had felt they had the boardwalk to themselves. Now, people were lined up for everything. The boardwalk was most crowded at the Hunt's Pier Starlight Ballroom. The attraction lights beckoned, and he could clearly read the neon signs of the nearby Flyer roller coaster and myriad rides that spun and swung. The sounds of the rides and games along Hunt's Pier enticed like a pied piper's tune. He thought of his original plan to surprise Althea with tickets to ride the Golden Nugget, and the larger roller coaster on the next pier. He moved to a bench, stood on the seat, and looked around. The Golden Nugget's stucco façade rose two stories high, and he could just hear the screams from the riders when the runaway mining car emerged from and quickly reentered the ride.

He hopped off the bench, dodged the crowd, and spotted a little stand that sold Philly cheesesteaks. He ate standing there, and washed the sandwich down with a Coca-Cola. Guy watched as fathers and mothers bought strips of tickets, and he smiled at how the children grabbed at them. He heard one plump boy yelling, again and again: "Another ticket, another ticket." Guy suddenly wondered how much money Althea would need to buy the wedding dress fabric, and as he disposed of the empty cheesesteak wrapper and cup, he wished he had not bought the sandwich.

He looked around and considered which of the boardwalk jobs he could do. He had never done any work outside of the farm where he'd grown up, and even then, his uncle had generally given him the simple, physical jobs anyone with a strong back could do. Mostly he had picked apples, and as he looked around at the fry cooks and the ride operators, he just couldn't picture himself working like that.

He found the nearest stairs to the beach, descended, and took a seat on the sand. The waves were barely visible, and rendered inaudible beneath the noisy commotion of the boardwalk. He remained there for a while, and then he picked himself up and walked under the boardwalk. He had to duck at times, but he managed to make it through the underpass of beams and found himself on Juniper Avenue.

He was easily a mile from the Skylark, and as he walked, he took note of the motels, to keep his mind occupied. He passed the Starlux Motel, the Fantasy, the Rio. He wondered how much, exactly, the nice rooms cost, and how people afforded them. There was the Sea Kist, Jay's Motel, and the Ocean Crest. The line of neon signs stretched on and on, each motel bustling with couples and families.

He began to recognize his surroundings, and knew he was near the Satellite Motel. He had walked and walked and finally thought he was too close to Max's apartment to stop.

When he arrived at Max's door, Guy heard laughter, and he contemplated whether to bother knocking. He heard Max say something inside the apartment, and then the door opened. Max practically pushed him down the stairs.

"Guy," he said, "I was just going out to get a big pie at Mack's. Never mind; it can wait. Come on in."

Max closed the door behind them, and they joined Althea and Jeannie at the table. Jeannie put her hand on Althea's.

"You look tired, Althea. Do you want Max to drive you home with Guy?"

Althea pulled her hand back. The four of them sat there. An alley cat came in through the open window, and Jeannie recognized it and waved it away with a nonchalant shooing motion. The cat purred at her, and curled its orange tail against everything it passed. It sauntered across the apartment, and Max rose, opened the front door, and ushered the cat out.

"Althea," Guy said. "Listen. I know you want a proper wedding dress and a proper wedding."

Althea looked up at him. She smiled faintly.

"It was my idea, Althea, to elope. And I know things haven't gone . . . well."

Althea reached to the center of the table and brought a magazine toward her. She felt her face swell with blood.

"We have a place to stay, Althea. You don't have to rush and do all this tonight. Why don't we go back to the motel?"

Althea stood, crossed to the credenza, and came back with an armful of thread spools. She dumped them onto the table and spread them out.

"Jeannie and I are choosing the shade of white I want from these threads. Then we'll order the fabric." She held a spool up to the light. "Did you know there were so many shades of white?"

"No," Guy said, "I didn't."

Jeannie and Althea continued to go through the spools. Max stood and twirled his keys.

"Jeannie's going to help me shop for some things, too," Althea said.

Guy started to speak, but stopped himself. He turned and walked to the door.

"I'll take Guy home," Max said.

It was past ten when Althea knocked on the motel door.

"It's unlocked," Guy said.

Althea opened the door slowly, entered, and sat on the chair near the window.

"Close the door."

Althea kicked the door closed. "That wasn't very ladylike of me," she said.

Guy put a pillow behind him so that he could see her clearly from the bed.

She stood up and came over to him. He sat up, placed his hand behind her head, and softly pulled her to him. Althea had dabbed behind her ears with one of Jeannie's perfumes, and Guy smelled it as he kissed her softly on the nape of her neck.

"I love you," she said.

Guy pulled back and looked at her. Althea's eyes looked almost kaleidoscopic in the scant light from the lone bulb in the bathroom. He pulled off the T-shirt he was wearing, and she placed her hand there on his chest, right near his heart. She splayed her fingers and rubbed firmly at the hairs on his chest.

Guy sat up and unbuckled his belt. He watched intently as Althea removed her clothes. She reached around and unhooked her bra, and he stared in the dim light at the erectness of her nipples. Holding her bra to the side, Althea let it go and arched her back. She ran her hands up through her long hair and let it fall.

He reached for her, and together their hands enveloped her breasts. Together, they moved her onto her back. He hovered over her. She reached to him and began to pull down his pants, and he found her hands with his.

A truck horn blared in the parking lot. There was the sound of air brakes releasing, and then the horn again. It startled him. She saw that his eyes had closed, and there was a tightness in his face. He pushed away from her and went to the drapes.

"What is it?"

"I don't know," he said. "Just somebody being a moron out there."

She turned her head to face him.

"Make love to me," she said.

Guy took a seat in the chair.

"I can't."

"Don't you love me?"

Guy dug his fingers across his scalp. "You know that I do."

Althea sat up and found her bra. "This is our *wedding* night," she said.

"No it isn't."

"We're as good as married, and you know that."

Guy pulled the drape back and looked out into the night.

"I said that too, before. That we were already married. I shouldn't have."

Althea walked quickly into the bathroom. Guy heard the shower come on. He pulled the drapes completely open, sat down, and stared outside.

The morning light entered the room at seven. The couple shifted and rubbed at their eyes.

"I forgot to close the drapes," Guy said.

Althea had gone to bed with her hair still wet, and it had set into a nasty tangle. She found her brush and went into the bathroom, closing the door soundly behind her. Guy got dressed, crossed to the bathroom door, and lifted his hand to knock. He stopped himself, turned, and left without saying a word.

When she emerged from the bathroom, Althea dressed and walked over to the Wildwood Diner. She had enough change on her for a coffee. The walk to Max's apartment was a long one, and had it been later in the morning she would have called Jeannie and Max for a ride. She figured they were probably still asleep. Max might have even gone off to work.

The walk passed quickly. Althea thought the walk similar to long drives in the early morning. Somehow, the time just went by more easily.

Max was descending the stairs when she arrived, and he gave her a friendly wave as he passed. When Althea reached the top of the stairs, she found the apartment door open.

Jeannie, seated at the kitchen table, lifted her mug in the air. "Cup?"

"No thanks," Althea said.

Jeannie set down the cup and motioned that they sit on the floor. She pulled over a small cedar chest, opened it, and removed dozens of wedding pamphlets and magazines.

"I had forgotten all about these," she said. "Max brings them to me when he goes to New York." She spread the magazines in a circle across the carpet, and Althea ran her hands over them, lightly touching the faces that graced the covers. "The pictures are what we need."

"Need?"

"Yes. We can get ideas for your makeup, hair, and jewelry."

Althea picked up a magazine and rifled through it. "Beautiful," she said.

Jeannie pulled an empty hatbox off a shelf and set it down on the floor. She found two pairs of scissors in the drawer and gave one to Althea. Together, they cut out the pictures they most liked and began to fill the hatbox.

"We'll narrow things down later," Jeannie said. "Maybe we can decipher some of these photos and figure out what materials they've used. We could even make you some clothes for the *boudoir*."

After a while, Jeannie got up and went to the pantry. She moved some boxes of cereal around, and then put her hands on her hips.

"What are you looking for?"

"I'm hungry for something sweet," Jeannie said. "I'll go get us a coffee cake at the bakery. You stay here and finish cutting. I can't wait to start *deciding* on things."

Althea nodded and picked up another magazine, cutting and adding pictures to the hat box. Her legs, tucked up under her, were getting sore. She rose, stretched, and began a slow walk around the quiet apartment. Next to the bed, on a shelf on the little table, she found a turquoise jewelry box. She opened it and picked at the necklaces inside.

One item she could not resist was a string of pearls. Althea squatted in front of a small mirror and encircled her head with the white pearls. The necklace clasped easily.

Althea heard a meow and faint scratching noise. She rose, smiled, and opened the door. She looked down at the cat that gracefully entered—and a pair of pointed brown dress shoes appeared and startled her.

"I'm afraid the cat beat me to the buzzer," the man in the brown shoes said. "My apologies."

He was a very tall man, older, and Althea wondered if he was the landlord.

"Is this your house, sir?"

"It is neither mine nor yours," he said. He took off his hat. "I am here to see Max. Is he about, my dear?"

Althea shook her head.

"Perhaps Miss Jeannie is present? In the loo?"

"She went out for a coffee cake." Althea held the door open, and the cat meandered in and out of the apartment.

"I believe I know that particular piece of jewelry," the man said.

Althea's hand quickly found the necklace. She blushed.

"Quite alright," he said. "I'm sure Miss Jeannie wouldn't mind you wearing it, yes?"

Althea moved her fingers along the strand of pearls. "I can't find the clasp."

"If you'll allow me," he said. He took a step into the apartment, and Althea retreated in kind.

"My apologies, again," he said. "I should be introducing myself rather than approaching you with my hands stretched forth."

The sound of shoes on the distant steps caught their attention and a voice called out. The man turned and peered down the staircase.

"Ah. Miss Jeannie is likely back with the cake," he said.

Jeannie took the last flight by pairs, and nearly lost the cake box as she threw her arms around the man.

"Sam," she said. "I haven't seen you in so long!"

Althea grabbed the precarious cake box from Jeannie's hand. She took it hurriedly to the table, and used the little time she had to remove the necklace. It caught a bit in her hair, and she pulled until it worked itself free. She just managed to get it and the jewelry box stowed away before Jeannie broke the embrace.

"Althea! This is our good friend, Sam."

"How do you do?"

"I do well," he said.

Althea gave him her hand, and he lightly kissed it.

They gathered around the table, and Althea kept watch on the man, wondering if he would tell Jeannie that she had been wearing the pearls.

"Sam," Jeannie said, "is a colleague of Max's."

"We work together, now and again."

Althea started to ask what they did, but decided the quickest way to get him out of the apartment was to remain quiet. She picked up a fork and broke off a piece of the cake. She ate, then broke off another.

"This one is a good eater," Sam said. "I like a woman who eats!"

Jeannie laughed and nudged Sam with her elbow.

"This is a pleasant visit," he said. "But as Max is not here, and you have such lovely company I would be remiss not to say my good-byes early."

"But you just got here."

"Another time," he said. "Please, don't get up."

He stood, replaced his hat, and made his way to the door.

"I see that pesky cat will not give up his—or her—feline plot to claim this abode."

He tipped his hat and pulled the door closed behind him.

Max entered the apartment and found Althea and Jeannie hard at work. They were sitting at the table writing down figures, and neither noticed Max until he cleared his throat.

"Max," Jeannie said, "I've finally done it. I've convinced Althea to go all out on a wedding dress."

"She has. And flowers, and even a musician playing the guitar."

Max crossed his arms. He looked at them for a moment.

"Max," Jeannie said, "Sam came by. I think he was very sorry he missed you again."

Max came over and joined them at the table. He picked up the papers with the figures on them.

"Guy's gonna need to make some real bread to pay for this," he said.

Jeannie smiled at Althea, then turned and made a face at Max.

"What?"

"Nothing," Jeannie said.

Althea stood and gave Jeannie a squeeze on the shoulder.

"You don't have to leave," Jeannie said.

"I should go. Guy will be worried."

She gathered her shoes, put them on, and waved goodbye. Jeannie and Max were bent over a piece of paper writing something down, and didn't seem to notice.

Outside, it was sunny, and she waited a minute for her eyes to adjust. It was a long walk back to the Skylark, and she barely had any money with her. She occupied herself with thoughts of the new wedding plans and the promise of the honeymoon.

The Fleur de Lis Motel lobby was air-conditioned, and she contemplated stopping in for a minute. She knew she should try to find Guy and tell him her new plans for the wedding. He was likely out looking for work, and she figured there had to be some kind of job center.

No one was at the desk of the Caribbean Motel, and so she tried at the nearby Ocean Crest. She waited for a few minutes while the woman working the desk talked endlessly on the phone. She grew impatient and decided to keep walking in the direction of the Skylark.

She moved determinedly, but did pause to peek in each time that she passed the kind of shop or food stand that might have hired Guy. Guy was somewhat taller than most men, and she slowed and looked across the sea of faces, but could not spot him anywhere.

It wasn't until Althea reached the Skylark's parking lot that she realized she was without a key. She walked the short distance to the Wildwood Diner. At the counter, she ordered a Coca-Cola and worriedly counted her change. She drank the cola slowly through a straw, and then ordered another.

When she exited the diner, she felt her pulse quickened by the soda pop, and found herself wondering what she might do with the rest of the day.

As she approached their motel room, she noticed a chair propping open the door. Attached to the chair she found a note from Guy. The note said simply that he was sorry.

Guy set his newspaper down on the table softly, but it stirred Althea nonetheless. She opened her eyes far enough to see him changing his madras shirt.

"You're back," she said.

"For a moment, I am," he said.

Althea closed her eyes and rolled away from the light that streamed in around the drape.

"I won't be long," he said. He didn't wait for her to acknowledge him. Once outside, he followed Surf Avenue north. As he passed Laura's Fudge, he inhaled the sweet aroma and suppressed a smile. He walked past the Packard and the 24th Street Motel. He turned east at the LeMarque Motel and fell in step with the boardwalk traffic.

After the boardwalk ended, he walked the remaining few blocks to his destination, his fresh shirt heavy with sweat. Inside the Trylon Motel, he rang the desk bell, and after what seemed like too long, a woman met him there. She told him the advertised position had already been filled. She wished him luck.

He had seen few open jobs in the newspaper, and here he was now, at the edge of the island. It seemed to him that he had looked in every window he passed. There was nothing to be had.

Althea woke first the next morning, and left to secure two cups of coffee from the lobby. The woman working the lobby had just brewed it, and remarked to Althea how delighted she was to have a young couple honeymooning with them. She had red lipstick on her teeth, and Althea fixated on it as the woman spoke. When Althea was done pouring the coffee, she thanked the woman, and tried to hide her ring-less left hand from view as she exited the lobby.

Althea and Guy sat at the table and sipped at their coffee.

"I think I figured something out," he said. "I think to get work in this town you have to know someone."

Althea nodded.

"Well, the only person I know is Max."

Althea blew on her coffee.

"So I'm going to ask him to help me."

"Okay. That's a good idea. I do want to show you what Jeannie and I are planning for the wedding. We will have a *real* wedding, then?"

"Of course, Althea. It's important to you. It wasn't really fair of me to take that away." Guy finished his cup.

"But I still am glad we *eloped*," he said. Althea nodded and smiled. "We'll get it together."

"Okay," she said. "You know I always planned to get married back home, with everyone there. Everyone who mattered."

He stood up and kissed the top of her head. "*We're* all that matter," he said. "And this is home."

There was a knock on the door. Althea pulled the drape back.

"Who's out there?" Guy asked.

"It's Jeannie," Althea said.

Guy turned the lock and opened the door.

"No need to come in," Althea said. "I'm already ready."

Althea followed Jeannie into the backseat of Max's car. Max honked the horn. They sat there, and Althea soon realized Max was honking for Guy.

"One minute," Guy shouted. Althea watched as he sat in the chair outside their room and put on his shoes.

"Shake a leg," Max said.

Guy got into the front seat, next to Max. He stared straight through the windshield as they pulled out. Max drove fast, and the long walk that Althea and Guy were so used to became simply a quick blur of time.

In the apartment's parking lot, Max spun his tires a bit for effect. He came to an abrupt stop, and the backseat emptied. Guy stayed put.

The men watched as Jeannie pulled Althea along to the back door of the building.

"I need to make some money," Guy said.

Max laughed and punched Guy in the shoulder. "Man, you have no idea how much money you need to make to foot the bills that girl of yours is going to be piling up."

Guy forced a smile.

"I do have a gig that needs a second hand . . . "

"Great," Guy said. "I don't have experience doing much of anything, though. Except farm work."

"Man, I don't know about farm work, but we can make you some money."

Max pulled out of the lot and headed south on Pacific Avenue. They passed Fern, Palm, Lotus and Myrtle, Primrose and Orchid. Guy thought about how Althea had taken note of all the streets in Wildwood that had flower names. It hit him why she took interest. He felt stupid for not having remembered with Althea.

"Althea's name means 'the rose of Sharon.'"

Max looked at Guy.

"Like these streets. They all have a flower name."

Max laughed. He hung a fast right on Saint, and then followed it on as it wound south again along the marsh. The car slowed, and Max peered around. It seemed to Guy that he was looking for something.

They parked the Hawk under a sign that read, 'Railroad Avenue.' Max turned off the ignition and got out. He disappeared for a moment behind some haphazardly parked cars in a makeshift parking lot. Guy heard a car start and watched as Max drove up to the Hawk's bumper in a black Ford.

Max waved from behind its steering wheel. He left the Ford running, got out, and disappeared again behind the parked cars. This time he drove out in a shiny pink Cadillac. He pulled the Cadillac alongside the Hawk and motioned for Guy to get out. Guy walked around to the passenger side of the Cadillac.

"Max. What are you doing?"

Max smiled and pointed to the Ford. "You're driving that one," he said. He revved the motor, and the pink Cadillac shimmied and rocked.

"Where are we going?"

"Wealthy guy I know wants me to drive his Cadillac up to Atlantic City."

Guy focused on Max's eyes. Max grinned and gunned the motor.

"So why didn't he just drive it up there himself?"

"He sailed his boat."

"On the ocean?"

Max put his hands in the air, palms skyward.

"It just sounds weird, Max. Why do you need a second hand anyway?"

"What are you, writing a book, Guy? The man has a yacht. He sailed up with his wife. Now I'm taking his Caddy up to him and *I need a ride back*. Get it?"

Guy turned and looked at the still-running Ford.

"So why this one?"

Max laughed again. "You think I'm letting you drive my Hawk?"

Max dropped the Cadillac into gear.

"Okay, Max. I'll help."

"Follow me, then. We'll be up and back in no time. And I'll split the money with you."

Guy started to ask how much, but Max hit the gas and Guy had to scramble into the black Ford before he lost sight of him.

Jeannie and Althea were having cocktails when Max and Guy returned. The apartment was a mess—strewn with fabric and patterns. A dressmaker's dummy rested on the love seat.

Max tossed his keys on the bed and poured himself a drink. He turned to offer the bottle to Guy, but Guy waved it off.

Jeannie and Althea were playfully arguing about the proper length for a train, so Max and Guy settled in and sifted through Max's records.

"Biggest collection I've seen," Guy said.

"Been collecting since fifty-six."

Guy grabbed a stack of records and went through them one by one. He had never even heard of most of the artists. He looked at the photos and tried to learn some of the names along with the faces. Gary U.S. Bonds. The Diamonds. Dick Dale, on a label called Deltone. The Rays and The Fleetwoods and The Ames Brothers. He held up an album by Johnny Horton.

"That one's okay," Max said. "Not my favorite or anything." Max pulled the sleeve off a forty-five by an artist named Domenico Modugno.

"Just play something, waxy Maxie," Jeannie said.

"Jeannie thinks that's funny. She thinks these records are made out of wax."

"I can hear you, *Max*."

Max placed the record on the turntable and played it. Domenico sang beautifully in Italian, and Guy noticed Max trailed the singer by a second or two. He studied the way Max tried to catch a lyric to sing. After a minute Max gave up and turned down the volume on the phonograph, got up, and went to the table. Jeannie, and then Guy and Althea, joined him.

"Where'd you go today?" Althea asked.

"Nowheres," Max said. "Nowheres at all."

"Right," Guy said. "We just cruised around."

Max poured Guy a drink, but Guy shook his head.

"You're alright," Max said.

Althea patted Guy's hand. "Go on, Guy. Lighten up a little bit."

Guy took the drink and raised it in salute. He drank it quickly.

"Guy," Jeannie said, "back me up here. Don't you think Althea should have a long train? She has such long, beautiful hair and she could wear it down with a long train."

"I don't know," Althea said.

"She thinks it's nineteen-fifty-one and not nineteen-*sixty*-one," Jeannie said. "She thinks she should wear a *tea-length* dress."

"I do not! Jeannie, you are *terrible*."

Max slapped Guy on the back. "Girls," he said.

"Soooo. How did you two end up here anyways?"

"Don't mind Jeannie, guys. She's drunk as a skunk."

Guy stood and went to turn off the record player. The pick-up arm had skipped, and the stylus had caught in the turnout groove. It was driving him crazy.

"What I mean," Jeannie said, "is that I've never known any *elopers*. And I'm not drunk. I've had *one* cocktail."

Guy came back and sat at the table.

"I don't know if we want to get into all of that," Althea said.

"Why? Isn't it all kind of romantic?"

Althea nodded at Jeannie.

"She doesn't believe that it's really romantic," Guy said. "Not really."

Jeannie looked at Guy, and then at Althea.

"I've said something I shouldn't have," she said. "I always do that."

Althea put her hand on Jeannie's.

Max laughed and picked up the bottle of gin. He filled his glass high, then tried to refill the other glasses. Jeannie motioned with her free hand for him to stop.

Guy stood and put his hand on Althea's shoulder. She looked up at him.

"Yes, we really should go," she said. "I'm very tired."

Jeannie helped Althea find her tabulation pad, and Max apologized that he couldn't drive them home. He finished his tall glass of gin as he said it. "There's usually cabs at the bar a block over. Take it on me." He pulled out a five-dollar bill and handed it to Althea.

"Thank you," she said.

Althea and Guy went down the stairs quickly, and found a cab right where Max said it would be. By the time they reached their motel room, Althea was practically asleep.

The next morning, Guy went out for a paper and some pastries while Althea showered. On his way back, he went to the Skylark's office and picked up a rate card. He matched their room type to the price key. It was fifteen dollars a night. He threw the card away in the trash bin near the stairs.

Inside, Althea was still in the bathroom, getting dressed. Guy pulled off part of a breakfast roll and ate it. He crossed to the bathroom and slipped the door open.

"I need Max's phone number. Do you know it now?"

Althea wrote it down on some toilet paper with her blue eyeliner.

Max pulled up, and Guy closed his newspaper. He folded it and laid it on the metal chair.

"What's the news?"

"Not much," Guy said. Max popped the door, and Guy climbed into the Hawk. "There is one story you might like. It says in the paper that Chuck Berry just opened his own amusement park."

Max laughed. "Crazy!"

Guy thought about how pleased such a random bit of news could make Max. He wondered if he, personally, had ever been so happy about something so overwhelmingly small.

"Where?"

"In St. Louis."

Max laughed again. "What's it called?"

"*Berryland*," Guy said.

Max bobbed his head. He pulled the Hawk into a service station and a boy hopped off a crate and began to fill it. Max played with the radio.

"We'll go there sometime," Max said. "The four of us." He hung a couple dollars out the window, and the boy eagerly took them. "Stay out of the sun, kid."

Max fired up the Hawk and they drove up and down Pacific Avenue. It was early, but an occasional hot rod passed, flaring its tailpipes.

"You can't really drag here no more," Max said. "Cops won't hassle us for cruising as long as we don't drag for pinks." As he spoke, a silver hot rod rolled by, inches off the ground.

"That was a deuce," Max said. "I think, anyway. Sometimes people soup up a rip-off and fake it as a deuce."

Guy noticed he was making Max do all the talking. "Jeannie doing anything with Althea?" As soon as it was out of his mouth, Guy realized how odd it was to not know what his fiancée was doing.

"Naw, Jeannie's at her folks'," Max said.

"You going?"

"Me? No. A bundie like me isn't invited."

Max didn't laugh at this. Guy thought for a moment. He had no idea what a "bundie" was, but he assumed it wasn't a good thing in the eyes of Jeannie's parents. He started to ask Max if he himself was a bundie, but stopped.

Max swung a U-turn at Jefferson. They had nearly left Wildwood Crest, and people and businesses were fewer and fewer.

"Jeannie's dad is a real ass, *if* you ask me. Came and went as he pleased his whole damn life. Real tuned out. Dig?"

"I do," Guy said. "I mean, dig."

Outside the city limits, Max ratcheted up his speed, and the wind inside the convertible picked up. Guy rolled up his window.

"Sorry, man," Max said. "I don't like the top up so much." He slowed to the legal limit, and Guy put the window back down.

"I grew up—since my parents died—on a farm with my uncle."

"That's cool."

"I guess. But I didn't ever really travel. And I guess I didn't think the money thing through real well."

"Never enough money, Guy. *That* I know."

Guy looked out the window. "What I knew," he said, "was that I *loved* Althea."

"So you took your Sophie by the hand and you copped a breeze."

Guy looked at Max. Then he laughed.

"I like that one," he said. "I think I even *understood* that one."

Max laughed with him, and it took a moment before they recognized the sound of a police siren.

"Hang on," Max said.

He floored it. The Hawk took up a lower gear, and Max drove firmly, his eyes nearly locked on the rearview mirror. Guy angled his side view mirror. The police car was about four or five blocks back.

Max swung a hard left on Rambler Road and cut right on Lake. The Hawk picked up speed, and in the side mirror, the police car faded. They made the base of Ephraim Island. Max drove behind some brush and killed the ignition, and they both slunk down in their open-air seats.

It took more time than they imagined, but the police car, lights and sirens flashing, finally passed.

Max put the top up and drove more slowly than Guy thought possible. He drove in a low gear along Cardinal Road and then backtracked carefully to his apartment. They got out behind the building, and Max tossed Guy the keys.

"In the trunk is a cover."

Guy opened the trunk and removed the car cover. Max grabbed the apartment's garden hose and sprayed the hood. Then he came around and sprayed the exhaust system. Guy covered the Hawk, and Max took back his keys.

They hopped the fence and made their way to the beach. Guy looked back at the covered Hawk with every step. No one came.

It was dinnertime when Max and Guy came back to the apartment. They had spent their day swimming in the ocean, and their shorts were soaked and dripping. Jeannie shooed them onto the balcony to dry.

"I'm cooking dinner," she said. "This will keep you out of my way."

From the balcony, Max and Guy looked around the neighborhood. Guy thought he heard a siren.

"Why don't you go get Althea?" Jeannie said.

Max looked down at the covered Hawk, and then back at Guy. He pulled out his keys and rattled them.

"Sure."

"Guy, you stay here with me," Jeannie said. "I could use a little help, actually."

Guy went into the kitchen and stood next to Jeannie. He looked down to see if he was still dripping. Max came inside, put on a fresh wifebeater, waved goodbye, and left.

"Could you set the table, Guy? I'm too hungry to wait to eat."

"Okay, Jeannie," Guy said. "Do I set four plates?"

"Why not? I should have enough here if Max doesn't act like a pig." She smiled as she said it. Guy wondered if Jeannie and Max always had the kind of relationship they had now.

"I'd ask what you did all day, but I'm guessing Max washed his car and went swimming like he always does."

Guy nodded.

"I know people who have lived here all their lives that never go in the ocean. Don't you think that's odd?"

Guy set down the last of the plates. "That is strange."

They sat and ate, and Jeannie stopped making conversation. She got up once and fiddled with the radio, but she kept getting news and weather, and gave up.

When Max and Althea arrived, Guy was helping Jeannie wash the pots and pans.

"Althea!"

"Hello, Jeannie."

Jeannie dried her hands and she and Althea bussed one another on the cheek.

"I think we should decide on the material for your wedding dress," Jeannie said. "We should get that order in."

Max grabbed the serving bowl of spaghetti off the table and started eating meatballs with his fingers.

"Max! I swear you're straight out of *Blackboard Jungle*."

Max put the bowl down and found a plate.

"I know that movie," Guy said. Althea pushed him gently.

"You never *saw* that," she said.

"I know," he said. "I just remember it. I remember the Church's ruling."

Jeannie made a puzzled face.

"Catholic League," Althea said. "He couldn't see *anything*."

"It's just a guideline," Guy said.

Jeannie fixed a plate for Althea and sat her down next to Max. Guy stood next to Jeannie at the sink.

"*Just* a guideline? Every time a movie came out where *anything* happened, the Pope himself decided the movie wasn't . . . what was the word?"

"Appropriate," Guy said.

Althea took a bite of spaghetti. She nodded to Jeannie. Then she swallowed and dabbed at her mouth with a napkin. "And for who? How do they personally know *you*, Guy? Or *me*?"

"You don't get it," Guy said.

"Neither do I," Max said.

Althea took some more spaghetti and handed off her meatballs to Max.

"Well," Jeannie said, "I don't really care to watch many movies. I always liked the newsreels where they showed all the Kennedys, though.

And I really don't get all these people's fascination with the television."

Max laughed. "You're a queer one."

"Yes," Guy said. "Let's talk about our great *Catholic* president and his father and brothers."

"I'd rather talk about his *wife*," Jeannie said.

Althea put down her fork. Max finished a last meatball and stood up.

"Okay, Guy. I think it's time we let these *girls* work on that wedding dress."

Guy and Max headed toward the door. Guy turned to say goodbye, but Althea and Jeannie had already closed ranks, amidst talk of the wedding dress.

Outside the apartment, Max gave Guy a look.

"What?"

"Thinking," Max said. "You up for something?"

"Can I get my money from the Atlantic City thing?"

Max laughed. "You will."

"Okay. What is it?"

"Can you play dead?"

Guy shrugged.

"I mean can you keep quiet about stuff?"

"I guess."

They uncovered the Hawk and got in. Max started the engine and pulled out of the lot. He drove two blocks away and pulled into a parking space.

"How much money *do you really* want to make?"

Guy looked out the window at the passing cars.

"Here's what I have, Guy. And it pays good money."

Guy looked at him. "Go on."

"A guy I know needs his liquor bottles cut with water. No big deal. It's been going on in this town since prohibition." Max looked around, checked his mirrors. "I can do it by myself; done it before. But you need money and it's a quick, easy, less boring job with two people."

"I don't know, Max," Guy said. Max turned off the ignition. "Is it really something that's been around?"

Max laughed. "Look it up."

"How much?"

"How much did I say for driving the Ford to Atlantic City?"

"You didn't."

Max opened his wallet. He gave Guy a twenty.

"So even more for this job?"

Max nodded.

The job had gone quickly with two, and Max paid Guy thirty dollars as soon as they were done. They had pilfered one bottle of gin, and Guy cracked it open while Max drove.

"Still pretty strong," Guy said.

"That's the key. In a bar you'd never even suspect it was cut."

Guy handed the bottle to Max. Max took a drink, and then another. Then he sealed the cap and stowed it under his seat. "That's already too much. The girls'll wonder what all we've been up to out here."

Max parked the Hawk behind the apartment building. They stepped back and looked up. Jeannie and Althea were outside on the balcony. They shined flashlights down on Max and Guy.

"You've been drinking," Jeannie said.

"That's just a *likely* guess," Max said.

Max and Guy climbed the stairs like drunkards, exaggerating their movements and pushing one another. The door to the apartment was open, and they took their seats at the table. Jeannie was shuffling a deck of cards.

"Poker, anyone?"

"Let's just play hearts," Althea said.

Max elbowed Guy. "Romantic, this one."

"You have been drinking, then?" Althea asked.

Guy shrugged. He didn't look at her. "Listen," he said. "I'm going to tell you how Althea and I did *actually* get here. Since you already asked." He pulled all the cards in and made a scattered pile in front of himself. "She'll get mad at me, but it's the truth, and it's why we're here."

Althea sat up tall and crossed her arms.

"You don't have to tell us," Jeannie said. "Really. I shouldn't have even asked the question."

"Just say it, then," Althea said. She stared hard at Guy. Guy relaxed his face and returned her stare.

"Okay. I will." He pushed the playing cards into the center of the table.

"Althea's father marched in Washington, D.C., back in twenty-eight. You heard of this march? All the way down Pennsylvania Avenue?"

Max shook his head.

"It was like a protest?" Jeannie asked.

Althea got up and walked to the balcony. She put her back to all of them.

"No," Guy said. "Or I mean, I guess it kind of was *sort* of like a protest, in a really sick way."

Althea turned to face them. "Christ, Guy. Just say it."

Guy bit his lip. "I won't."

Jeannie stood up and went to Althea. She put her arm around her.

"My father was a Klansman," Althea said.

No one said anything for a minute. Althea put her head in her hands.

"Althea," Jeannie said. "It's okay. It's not *you*."

"Lot of people get into that," Max said.

Guy stood up. He went over to Althea. Jeannie gave her off and sat back down.

"Not like this," Guy said. "He was a ranking officer. Some kind of wizard, or whatever they call it."

"He wasn't a wizard," Althea said.

"Wasn't? Or *isn't*?" Guy asked.

"Enough," Althea said. "He's my *father*."

"I'm sorry, baby. I'm just saying that's why we're here."

Guy sat back down. "We couldn't marry back home. Her father would never allow it."

"I don't get it," Jeannie said.

Max walked to the far corner of the room and lit a cigarette. He fidgeted with it and used his hand as an ashtray.

"Are you . . . " Jeannie said, " . . . part *negro*?"

"No," Guy said. "I'm not."

"He's Catholic," Max said.

Althea put her hands on her head. She bent and shook her head and long hair up and down, obscuring her face. "It's all just so *damned* stupid and it's all my *damn* fault."

Max came back across the room and put his cigarette out under the faucet. "Parents aren't our fault," he said. "Trust me. It took me years to understand that."

"Max's dad was an asshole," Jeannie said. "Sorry. But he is."

Max put his hand up to her. "But not anymore," he said.

They let the conversation die.

When Guy and Althea awoke, it took them a minute to realize where they were. They had spent the night on a sleeping bag on the floor. Max had left a note that said he'd be back later.

While Guy used the toilet, Althea poured them each a bowl of Life cereal. There wasn't much milk, and the cereal sat hard in the bowls.

Max and Jeannie came back, and Max waved before grabbing the keys to his Hawk. "Guy," he said. "Make some dough?"

Guy took a mouthful of dry cereal and kissed Althea goodbye.

Max didn't tell Guy where they were going. They drove across town into North Wildwood. When they finally stopped, Max led them across a full parking lot to an unmarked steel door. He knocked, and the door instantly opened a foot or so. A shaggy-haired man peered out.

"Who the hell's *this* one?"

"This is my younger brother, Guy," Max said. "He's cool."

The man looked at Guy. "He don't look little to me."

"I didn't say he was little," Max said.

Guy crossed his arms and cocked his head to make himself look more like Max. The man didn't seem to be buying it.

"Alright, alright," the shaggy-haired man said. "Come on in anyhow."

Max stayed in line with the man, and Guy tried to keep up. With no knowledge of the layout, and the only low light coming from a distant room, Guy kept bumping into tables and chairs. He watched Max enter the room, reach up, and swing the lamp. Guy saw only a slice of the room through its door. He saw first a hand, and then a bag. Another man, this one older and carrying a cane, came out and stood in front of Guy. He lifted his cane and pointed it at Guy. Guy took a full step back.

Max emerged from the room and pushed past the man with the cane. Guy followed Max outside, and the sun stung their eyes. They walked quickly, looking at the ground as their eyes adjusted. Max got in the Hawk and placed the bag he had picked up on the passenger seat. As Guy moved to open the door, Max locked it.

"Not you," he said. He looked around and started the engine. "Walk around for a few minutes, Guy. Maybe hang out on the boardwalk and watch the tourists go by."

" . . . Then what?"

"Then," Max said, "come back here and do exactly what I just did."

He gunned the engine, then dropped into gear and drove up Wildwood Avenue. Guy watched him turn right on Atlantic and disappear.

Guy walked the long, slow block to Laura's Fudge and stared into the window. The taffy machine was working, and he watched it stretch and turn and pull the bright, red candy. He looked around, and slowly meandered back to the metal door.

It took a minute before anyone answered his knock. The man with the shaggy hair appeared and pulled Guy inside. He closed the door and locked it. Guy felt his heartbeat pick up.

"You came back a little too soon," the shaggy-haired man said. Guy nodded.

The man walked over to a nearby poker table. An overhead light was on, now, and Guy saw hundred-dollar bills scattered across the table. The man counted the money into a bag, and when he finished, he pulled out a fifty dollar bill.

"This is for you," he said.

Guy watched as the man folded the bill tightly into a square and tucked it into Guy's shirt pocket.

"Don't touch the rest of the money. Got it?"

Guy nodded. The man handed him the bag and moved to the metal door. He unbolted the door and opened it, and the light sliced across the room.

"I go this way," he said. "You go up the stairs and out the front."

Then he left, slamming the steel door behind him.

Guy placed the money bag under his shirt and looked for the stairs. When he reached the top floor he saw that he had entered a small Italian eatery. He looked through the front of the eatery to the boardwalk. None of the patrons seemed to notice as he casually strolled to the front exit. A woman working a soda fountain handed him a cup as he passed her.

"Drink this while you walk," she said. She jabbed a straw into the cup. "Real nonchalant. While you walk."

Guy took the straw between his lips and strolled out onto the boardwalk. He stood under an awning that blocked the bright sun, and drank the lemonade while he waited for his pupils to contract. As he finished the lemonade, he looked around for Max, but did not see him. Guy was a long way from the apartment, and he decided to head there.

When he arrived, he went to the back and looked for the Hawk. There was no sign of it. He walked to the front door of the apartment building and went in. The door closed behind him, and he stood there and thought about whether or not he should go up. He heard the building's front door swing open.

"You have my money," the man said. "Terribly wrong direction you took."

Guy turned and found himself facing a man much taller than himself.

"I am Sam," the man said. "And that is my money you have so cleverly *concealed* beneath your shirt."

Guy looked down, and removed the bag.

"You are an acquaintance of Max's?"

Guy nodded. "I'm his brother."

Sam laughed and held out his hand for the bag. "I'm afraid that is false," he said. "Though I wish that it were not."

A quick knock came at the door, and it opened a fraction of the way before it found Sam.

"Ah," he said, turning. "There is our mutual friend now."

He moved toward Guy so that Max could step into the crammed vestibule. Max grabbed the bag from Guy and handed it quickly to Sam. Sam shook his head at Max.

"A little sloppy, Max. But I am glad to have met your brother."

He gave Max a light slap on the cheek, turned, and left.

"What was all that, Guy?"

"You tell me, Max."

Max slapped Guy across the back. "You were supposed to make a *drop*."

"A drop?"

Max tried to find a nonexistent cigarette behind his ear. "A drop. You know. Someone takes the bag the rest of the way."

"I don't 'dig' this," Guy said. He sat down on the steps, and Max joined him.

"Relax. No big deal. It's just the house picking up their cut of a poker game." Max patted Guy's shirt. He found the fifty and pulled it out of Guy's pocket. "You dig *this*?"

Guy took back the fifty and put it in his wallet.

"Guy, you know how long it takes to earn *fifty* bucks, after taxes, slinging hash browns and eggs?"

Guy shook his head no, then yes.

"Okay, Max. But why'd you set me up like that?"

"I didn't. They were supposed to tell you where to make the drop. That guy with the hair, he's an addict. He'd forget his own head."

Max turned and ascended the stairs. Guy waited a minute, then followed.

Althea was wearing her wedding dress with Jeannie's pearl necklace when Guy walked in. She wore Jeannie's white heels and her long blonde hair was pulled up and styled.

"You look beautiful," Guy said.

She smiled at him. She'd applied pink lipstick, and Jeannie had curled up her eyelashes and touched them with soft, black mascara.

"We're just practicing here," Jeannie said. "While we're working on the new wedding dress, we thought we'd fiddle with her hair and jewelry and makeup."

Althea put her hand to her mouth and blew kisses at Guy.

Max waved and eventually caught Guy's attention. He rubbed his fingers together like money.

The next day, Jeannie decided to go through Althea's things to see what they could find for her something old and her something blue. Althea asked Guy for some money to buy something new. He gave her twenty dollars. She was "over the moon" that the wedding was coming together, and she told him so again and again.

Max took Guy to a construction site off St. Paul Avenue. When they stepped out of the Hawk, a few people yelled, "There he is," and, "Hey, Maxie!"

Max went over and shook hands with a few of them, then pointed back at Guy. He came back to the Hawk and pulled a notebook and pencil from the glove box. "You up for some easy money?"

Guy nodded. Max opened the notebook and found the right page.

"This is self-explanatory," he said. "You just take down the name and the amount, and the team they want to wager on. This is even Stephen betting. No spread. Easy."

"Baseball games?"

Max slapped Guy on the back. He got in the Hawk and drove away.

After he had filled the book and collected the money, Guy walked to the corner of Atlantic and Toledo and grabbed a cup of coffee at the Ala Kai Motel. He thought about calling the apartment, but figured that could go wrong. When he stepped out of the motel, Max was there waiting for him in the Hawk.

"How'd we do?"

"We did very well," Guy said.

Max took a zigzag route and they were back at the apartment in no time. When they came into the apartment, Jeannie could scarcely contain herself.

"We've decided on the beach," she said. "Right on the beach, for the wedding ceremony. What do you think?" Guy couldn't tell if she was talking to him or to Max.

"Sounds pretty cool," Max said.

"Max, Jeannie says you know some people who could rent us a big tent," Althea said.

Max looked at Guy.

"I think I need a drink," Guy said.

Max went to the refrigerator and tossed him a bottle of Miller High Life. "Girls? Do you want?"

Jeannie nodded at him, and he gave them each a bottle. He came back over to Guy.

"Finish that," Max said. "You and me have some more work to do."

Guy finished the beer and handed the empty bottle to Jeannie. He gave Althea a wave and followed Max out the door.

Max drove them to the same spot on Railroad Avenue where they picked up the Caddie. This time, Max put Guy in the passenger seat of the black Ford, and he took the wheel for himself. They drove for a while, then stopped for a burger at a diner outside of town. They ate extra fries and drank chocolate milkshakes, and Max footed the bill.

When they got back in the Ford, Max started the engine, then sat still for a minute, and fiddled with the radio.

"Wish I could tune in to that new DJ over in Philly. They call him the Geator with the Heator. Heard of him? He plays whatever he wants."

Guy said nothing. He put his window partway down and watched the trees go by as Max drove around on the outskirts of town. It was getting dark.

Althea wanted to go back to the motel. Jeannie told her it wasn't safe for a pretty girl like her to take a cab by herself at night.

"Why don't you just stay here, Althea? When Max and Guy get back, he'll drive you guys home."

Althea sat down on the edge of the bed.

"What's wrong, hon?"

"I feel . . . I don't know."

Jeannie picked up their shoes. "Let's go swimming."

"No way," Althea said. "I'm not going in the ocean in the dark."

Jeannie put on shoes and kicked Althea's to her. Althea put them on, and they went out. Jeannie led, and Althea reluctantly followed. They stopped a couple blocks into a motel district, and Jeannie pointed at a small, enclosed pool.

"We'll get kicked out, Jeannie. These pools say no swimming after sunset."

"Relax," Jeannie said. "No one's going to kick two pretty girls out of a pool."

They hopped a small fence and sat down on Adirondack chairs to untie their shoes. "Keep your bra and underwear on if you want," Jeannie said.

Jeannie stripped off all her clothes and dived in. Althea watched her sit on the bottom of the pool, and saw the bubbles Jeannie made float and pop on the water. Althea looked around. The motel rooms were mostly blocked from view by the plastic palm trees that lined the pool. Althea watched Jeannie surface. Finally, Althea removed her outer clothing.

"Is it cold, Jeannie?"

"No, actually it isn't all that cold. Come on in."

Althea put a toe in the water.

"Just jump in. Get it over with."

Althea came slowly down the steps. She watched as Jeannie effortlessly floated the length of the pool.

Max pulled the black Ford onto a patch of gravel. The surrounding thicket obscured bits of abandoned car parts and tires. Most of the vegetation had died. It looked to Guy like the edge of the universe.

"This is making me nervous, Max."

Max killed the engine. Then the lights. As his eyes adjusted, Guy made out a building in the distance.

"See that road?"

Guy looked ahead and squinted.

"Lean your head out the window."

Guy put his head out the window. He looked down at the gravel road that hugged the outside of the building.

"What I need you to do," Max said, "is drive this Ford along this road."

Guy looked at him and studied his face.

"When we get to the edge of the building, you'll stop the car."

"For what?"

"To wait." Max hunched forward, low, and lit a cigarette. He took a few quick drags from it and then put it out against the floorboard. "While I'm working, you'll drive along real slow. Creeping."

Guy looked again at the building. "What are you going to do?"

Max laughed. It didn't strike Guy as a normal laugh.

"Just a little fire, Guy. No big deal."

Guy opened his door and got out of the car.

"Get the hell back in, Guy. What's wrong with you?"

Guy got back in. He left the door open.

"What's wrong is I'm not going to burn anything!"

Max motioned for him to close the door. Then he reached across Guy and pulled the door slowly closed until it latched.

"Let's just go, Max. Take me back to your apartment."

"For what, Guy? So you can find out how much more money you need? Look, man. Get serious. Do you really want to get married and get a place and take care of her?"

Guy nodded.

"Then it's this. Okay? You'll make enough money tonight to do all of that." Max reached into his coat for another cigarette. He brought out his empty pack of Lucky Strikes and crushed it.

"How much?"

"What?"

"How much money are you going to give me?"

The police car rolled in with its lights going full tilt. Jeannie brought her hand up and told Althea not to get out. A beam of light shone in Althea's face and she edged herself to the side of the pool.

"Go under," Jeannie said.

They both went under and held their breath as long as they could before reemerging. Althea came up first, then Jeannie.

"Evening."

The officer shining the flashlight at Althea was young, and in full uniform. Althea focused on his holstered gun.

"Evening, yourself," Jeannie said.

The officer near Jeannie was older. He turned to the younger officer and smiled.

"What is the problem?" Jeannie asked.

The older officer shut off his light and knelt by the pool. "Seems it's a little dark out here for swimming," he said.

Jeannie looked up at the sky. "I hadn't noticed it had gotten dark."

"Says private property on the sign here as well."

"Does it?"

The younger officer walked over and pointed his light at the sign. Then he shut off the flashlight and tapped the sign with the butt end. Jeannie swam over to the ladder.

"That's far enough," the older one said.

"I'm tired of swimming."

"Then float," the younger one said.

The older officer dragged an Adirondack chair over. He purposefully scraped it along the pool's concrete deck, then stopped, and let the chair settle into place.

"Think I'll sit here," he said. "Better view."

He sat down and crossed his legs. Jeannie looked over at the younger officer. He had taken out a pad and was writing something down.

"I think I know you," she said.

The younger officer ignored her and kept writing.

"You have to tell me your name, by law," she said.

He stopped writing. Slowly, he walked over to Jeannie's side of the pool.

"Not sure what you think you're doing standing there *leering* at me," Jeannie said, "since you clearly know *who* I am."

"First of all, I am writing a report, not leering. Secondly, you mean who *Max* is."

The older officer laughed at the younger officer's comment, then stood tall and spoke to the people that had gathered on their balconies to watch. "Nothing to see," he said. "Go about your business."

Althea turned and looked up. She couldn't quite see the faces of the people watching.

The older officer turned on his flashlight. He aimed it, as best he could, at Jeannie's naked breasts.

About fifteen yards from the building, Guy took his foot off the gas pedal and let the Ford coast. He felt Max's weight leave the trunk. In the side mirror, he watched Max uncap a gas can.

"Keep it coasting," Max said. "Not too fast."

Guy slammed on the brakes.

"What the hell, Guy?"

Guy killed the engine. He watched Max set down the can and approach his window.

"I'm not doing this, Max."

Max came around to the passenger side and got in. "You're not John Doe, you know."

"I'm not John *anything*, Max."

Max opened the glove box. He pulled out a wad of cash, bundled and rubber-banded. He held it up.

"You wanted to know how much bread you'll get for this job. Right?"

Guy shifted in his seat, away from Max. "I'm not an arsonist."

Max undid the rubber band. Guy heard it snap, and then the shuffling of bills. “No one’s asking you to be an arsonist, Guy. I’m the arsonist.”

Guy turned his head and looked at the money in Max’s hands.

“How much, Guy?”

“There isn’t enough to get me to do this. *I’m* not a criminal.”

Max set the money on the dashboard. “Who do you think you are, Guy? All of a sudden? You think you didn’t commit a crime helping me transport that stolen Caddie?”

Guy winced. He turned and stared out his window.

“You think you didn’t already commit enough crimes with me to go to jail?”

Guy got out of the Ford. Max followed, and they met in front.

“I’m doing this job. Right now, Guy. You want to make a lot of money, or not?”

Guy pushed at him. Max took a step back.

“You can do the job without me. Why do you need me?”

Max took a seat on the hood. “I need a lookout, and I need someone to drive the car while I’m doing this.”

Guy walked toward the building. It looked vacant. Some of the windows were shattered.

“Look, Guy. You’re here *either* way. You want to make the money or not?”

“What if I just drive away?”

Max walked up and stood in Guy’s space. “What do you *think* might happen if you tried?”

Guy took a step back. He wondered if Max had a gun or a knife on him. An owl hooted in the distance. Everything about the abandoned building, the untended grounds, and the remoteness of the area made Guy think no one could be around to hear them. He thought of Althea, and how much he truly wanted to free her from her father.

“I want half, Max. You give me half what you’re getting, and I’m all in.”

Jeannie refused to get out of the pool.

“You there—Max’s girlfriend’s friend,” the younger officer said. “Why don’t you come on out now?”

Althea started to follow his direction, but stopped. “I’m not getting out until you throw Jeannie her clothes."

"Maybe," he said, "we should come in there, in the pool, and cuff you."

A camera bulb flashed, and Althea saw a woman sitting on top of a nearby VW, with a Kodak held up to her face.

"Knock that crap off," the older officer said. The bulb flashed again.

"Okay," he said. "Enough. Here's your things."

He kicked Jeannie's clothes into the pool. The younger officer picked up Althea's clothes and handed them to her.

"Thank you," Althea said.

Althea and Jeannie got dressed in the shallow water of the pool stairs, and then climbed up. They stood, dripping, at the edge of the stairs. Someone threw them a couple of towels from the balcony. The younger officer walked over to where they had landed and picked them up. Another flashbulb went off.

Guy finished peeing at the base of a buttonwood tree, then walked over and watched as Max counted out the money on the hood of the Ford.

"Here it is," Max said. "I counted it twice." He banded Guy's half and sent the money sailing across the hood. Guy searched for it in the dim light, spotted it, and picked it up off the ground.

"Let me count it," Guy said.

Max came over and snatched the money from him, then doubled back to place it in the glove box. "Now, let's get on with it," he said.

Max walked back around the Ford to his gas can. He picked it up and doused the corner of the building. A single, shielded bulb above him barely shed light, and Guy could just make out the fuel's rising vapors.

After a minute or so, Max had emptied all his gas. He left the can by the corner of the building and walked back to Guy.

"Get in and drive along the building. *Slow*."

Guy obeyed. He crawled the Ford along the side of the structure. In his side mirror, he watched as Max tossed glass jars from the trunk.

It was a longer building than Guy had thought. The glass jars kept smashing. As soon as Max got done with one, he picked up another. Everything reeked of fuel. Guy rolled up his window and reached across to put up the window on the passenger side.

"Keep it steady, Guy. Shit, man!"

Guy turned from the window crank and realized he was brushing the Ford across a deep hedge.

"Get to the garage opening," Max said.

The glass jars stopped popping. Guy felt Max shifting and moving around in the trunk.

"Stop here."

Guy put on the brakes. He felt Max's weight leave the trunk.

"Stay put, Guy. Just a minute."

In the side mirror, Guy watched Max pull at something in the trunk. Max disappeared completely into the trunk for a moment, then appeared again in Guy's mirror. He carried an enormous, red gas can. Guy thought it must hold five gallons, maybe more. He watched Max drag it toward the building, struggling with its weight.

Max opened the can and fed thick rope into it like a snake coaxed into a charmer's basket.

"Okay, Guy. In a minute, I want you to drive slowly around the building to the other side of the garage opening. Okay?"

Guy rolled down his window to hear better. "Okay."

"I'm going inside right here. You'll pick me up around the building on the opposite side. Drive slow. Watch your rearview mirror. And put off the lights. Okay?"

Guy nodded. Max closed the trunk softly.

"Keep looking ahead, into the woods. You see anything at all, you put it in reverse and come back to this spot fast to get me. Got it?"

Guy switched off the lights.

"See you in a minute," Max said. "Easy money. Just like I told you."

Guy released the brake and watched as Max took an end of the rope and went inside the building. Without the aid of lights, Guy had to move forward slowly, his head hanging out the window like a dog's.

Althea and Jeannie weren't speaking to one another in the police car. The younger officer drove, with Althea in the front passenger seat. Jeannie sat in the back, behind the driver, alongside the older officer. Althea thought it strange to be in police custody for swimming in a motel pool.

Jeannie had been handcuffed to her door, but Althea's hands were cuffed together in her lap. The young officer had been the one who cuffed her, and he had left the cuffs loose. She was free to move her hands around together, as a pair, but she kept them stationary.

Jeannie made movements in the back, and Althea fought the urge to turn to look at her. Occasionally the older officer would tell Jeannie to "just take it easy" and to "just settle down," and it was obvious to Althea from the noises that Jeannie was fighting with the door.

The young officer drove the police car in silence. He acted as if he knew exactly where he was going, but Althea slowly realized that they were going north to go west to go south to go east.

Outside the window, the night was quiet. Whenever they passed a restaurant in town, people would wave at or salute the police officers. Often Althea noticed cars slow down and let them pass. Eventually the younger officer pulled the car onto a familiar street, and Althea searched for her motel. When they got close to the Skylark, she turned her head slightly and looked past Jeannie through the rear window. The light in their motel room was off.

Jeannie had caught Althea's subtle turn. She pulled at her cuffs. "Althea, honey. You okay up there?"

Althea heard the older officer mumble something, and Jeannie stopped talking.

As Max's gas can disappeared from the mirror, Guy turned his focus to the woods ahead. He saw that the woods were stiff with pines. He focused so hard on the pines, in his effort to see anything at all, that he almost missed the curve of the road.

Guy heard a popping noise behind the car, and glanced in the rearview mirror as the trunk flung open. The lid bounced to its apex and then bobbed up and down as he drove. He had made the first curve left, and the second came fast—the building was long but quite thin—and he swung the wheel and hit the brakes.

He got out and came around to the trunk. The odor was overwhelming. He backed off for a few seconds and brought his shirt up to cover his mouth as he breathed. Without thinking, he placed his hand on top of the trunk and slammed it shut. The noise reverberated like a hunter's rifle. It echoed against the bluff.

In the distance he saw something move. The figure seemed too large to be Max, and the placement seemed wrong.

The figure split in two. Half moved to the left and disappeared. Guy watched the other figure grow larger, more defined.

He squatted down to blend in with the black Ford. Keeping his chest in contact with the metal, he moved to the passenger side and scooted up to the fender. He used the side mirror to partially obscure his head, and rose. He could now see the larger figure standing, looming in the distance.

The passenger window was only halfway up, and he managed to get his arm inside. The glove box gave with a small click, and he rooted around for the money Max had taken. He pulled the first object he found and brought it slowly out the window. It was a blackjack. For a moment, he considered putting the leather-wrapped lead bar in his pocket. He turned and looked in the direction of the woods. The bluff was close, there in the dark.

He heard more noises in front of the Ford, and saw light. He brought his head up high enough to get a better look. The figures had come from a car, and he saw its headlights point into a recess in the building. The light filled nearby windowpanes.

Guy reached his arm back into the Ford. He placed the blackjack on the seat and found the glove box. He ran his hand along the inner top of the glove box, and then down. With a swift motion, he yanked the contents out. There was a brief smatter of noise against the seat. Guy raised his head again. A flash of light swung off the building and filled the cabin of the Ford.

His hand shook. The metal of the car was cold. He pushed his body and face into it as if to fuse with the vehicle. The light retreated. He peered over the window. The small band of money Max had taken from him was there, with Max's larger wad attached as well.

In a quick burst of movement, he stood, reached into the Ford, and grabbed all the money with both hands. He took Max's leather jacket as well, and then lurched back. He stood and quietly stuffed the money into Max's jacket, and put it on. For a moment, he did not feel scared.

He heard a scuffling noise in the distance, and a small cloud of dust rose and swam in the headlights. One of the figures entered the car, and then, a swirl of police car rotators filled the darkness.

Guy stumbled. He tried to right himself, but his feet kept moving backward, in a freakish rhythm. He knew that if he fell, they would hear him. He stopped and allowed himself to breathe.

In the distance, the dust had settled, and Guy saw an officer forcefully handling Max. The other officer lit up the building with a lamp light attached to the police car.

Guy turned and ran. He ran as fast as he could in the dark, and the jacket bounced unmercifully. The wad of money in its pocket threatened to break free. He placed his hand over it. The bluff kept its distance. Guy increased his pace. Every time he felt he would make its break, it moved on him. He thought he saw a sweep of light across its undergrowth. As he reached the dense thicket of pines, Guy doubled over in exhaustion.

The young officer pulled the police car into the precinct lot and shut off the engine. Before he could remove the keys, Jeannie spoke.

"This isn't necessary."

The older officer took off his cap and ran his fingers across his scalp. Althea watched him rest his hand on Jeannie's leg. "You cops want me, not Althea."

The older officer turned from Jeannie to look at Althea. Althea turned away.

"We don't want her? Why not?"

"No," Jeannie said. "You don't. What's the point? She's got no record. She'll take up your time doing paperwork and she'll leave here with a warning."

The younger officer looked to the older one. Then he pulled the keys out of the ignition, put them in his pocket, and turned to Althea. "That true?"

The older officer placed his right hand on Althea's shoulder and squeezed.

"It's true," Althea said.

He removed his hand from her shoulder. "But not you, Jeannie," he said. "We can't say your record's clean, can we?"

The younger officer pulled his keys back out of his pocket and reached into Althea's lap. She pulled away, and he stopped. He moved slowly, with the key showing, and undid her cuffs.

"Thank you," she said.

The older officer leaned into Jeannie. He kept his hand on her leg. "Not so fast," he said.

He put his finger on his cheek and tapped. Jeannie brought her mouth over to kiss him. He turned at the last instant and caught Jeannie's lips with his. Althea watched as the older officer both protruded and flicked his tongue.

The younger officer opened Althea's door. She could smell his aftershave as he reached across her.

Althea did not look at anyone as she exited the car. She walked a few steps, but then turned and watched as the officers led Jeannie into the police station. She started to follow them, but the younger officer saw her, raised his hand, and waved her off.

Guy wished he smoked. He knew if he were a smoker he would likely have matches he could light and burn. As it was, he could scarcely see his hand in front of him. The tangle of underbrush was thick and unforgiving. No path seemed better than another.

He remembered that Max smoked. He felt into every pocket and crevice of the jacket. Nothing. He thought if he found the Zippo, he could make a torch out of his shirt. Then he thought of what little good it would do. The brush was too thick, and the torch would burn out before he made it thirty feet.

If the police had followed him, they would use their lights. He could stay low and pick his way through the illuminated brush. He kept moving forward. He stumbled and caught his feet in tangles of exposed roots again and again, and there was a nasty, thorny briar that kept finding him. It cut at him and held, and he had to kneel constantly to extract himself.

He stopped and listened. The police clearly were not coming for him. If he could just hear the sound of a tire on distant pavement, he believed, he could follow it. There was no such noise, not even an owl or a hawk or a rodent.

The image of Max, of his shadowy figure with the police, came to Guy's mind. He wondered whether the police knew there had been an accomplice. Max might not have said anything. Guy knew he had to keep moving. Althea was likely with Jeannie, and soon Max would be calling and everyone would wonder: *Where is Guy?*

He kept moving. He was tripping less, and his feet began to take full steps beneath the massive pines.

He could be going in the wrong direction, and he knew it. The canopy above was simply too thick for him to find and follow a star. He tried to blaze forward in a continuous straight line. If he did so long enough, he knew he would eventually find his way out.

Then he heard water. He would reach water and it would be too deep, too rocky to cross. He would have to go back to the crime scene. To the police, and to jail.

Then he heard the rushing again. It wasn't water, he realized—it was the sound of pliable rubber on asphalt.

It didn't take Althea long to reach the boardwalk. She ran and jogged most of the way there, a mixture of anger and fear fueling her. She ran down the middle of the streets to avoid the drunkards, the derelicts. A slight drizzle misted the air.

Once on the boardwalk, she felt safe. She was out of breath and walking as fast as she could along the beach side. She caught up to a tramcar and stayed with it as it parted the way.

The image of the older officer putting his tongue in Jeannie's mouth came to her. She felt a shiver run up her spine, and shook almost uncontrollably. Her stomach felt ill.

The tramcar stopped short, and Althea practically landed in its backseat. She put her hands up to brace herself, and her fingers brushed the face of the man sitting there. The contact startled her, and she jumped aside.

She tried to run the rest of the way to the Skylark, but the illness she felt curtailed her. She took the nearest ramp off the boardwalk and stayed on whichever side of the street was most illuminated by street lamps. Families passed her. At every step, she felt their stares.

Finally, at their motel door, she reached for the key. It wasn't on her. She turned the knob and pushed, and the door somehow gave. She switched on all four of the room's lights and locked the door.

The water was warm as she ran the spigot. She wanted to take a bath and wash off the night, before Guy came home. Her body still flinched with the chill that came from running and sweating on such a cool night.

She entered the shallow bath, using her palms to steady herself. Her body covered itself in chill bumps, and she scooped at the water as best she could in an effort to cover her legs and get warm. A towel dangled near her, and she grabbed it and set it up like a pillow behind her head.

Guy wondered if what he heard had been, not a tire on a road, but thunder in the distance. He could hear an occasional rumble in the direction he walked. If it was indeed cars Guy was hearing, he knew he could easily hitch a ride back to the Skylark. Then he would have to locate Althea and make a plan.

A light flashed in the distance, but the thunder that he expected to follow never came. Guy stopped and looked around. If the police had been tracking him, they could have caught up. The light flashed again.

He walked toward where he had seen the splash of light. If the police had circled all the way around, he knew, they had him. He was too tired to turn and pick his way back through all the brush.

The brambles suddenly increased in density, then petered out into a clearing. The light splashed the mowed grass in front of him, and he kept walking toward it. A final pair of trees stood before him, and he broke free—and there before him was blacktop.

No lights, no cars were around, and for that he was momentarily happy. He sat at the edge of the road and took his shoes off. He gave himself a minute to rub his swollen feet before he replaced and loosely retied his shoes. His hands bore visible scratches, as did his legs, and he placed his fingertips against the painful stings on his face.

He felt Max's jacket for the wad of cash. It was secure. He patted the smaller pocket for the lighter money. It was still there, too.

A light flashed and illuminated the entire stretch of blacktop.

Guy stepped fully into the road. The vehicle stopped. A woman sat still in the passenger seat. Guy came over and peered inside. An older man gripped the steering wheel. Two children argued in the back.

"Are you okay?" she asked.

Guy nodded. He looked down at his cut legs. The woman looked down as well.

"I got lost in the woods."

"Where are you going, dear?"

"Wildwood."

The woman turned and said something to the man.

"Wrong way," the man said.

Guy stepped back and watched the car drive off. The next few cars headed that same way. He decided to walk in the other direction. It was cool enough that he was happy to have Max's jacket. He flipped up the collar.

When the truck came, he felt its vibrations on the road before he saw any lights. The driver slowed to a stop, and Guy stopped walking and turned to face the truck.

"Gonna get yourself killed, son!"

"Yes, sir," Guy said.

The man had opened the door, and Guy climbed the short stepladder into the front cab. The cabin smelled immeasurably of fuel.

"Wildwood, son?"

"Yes, sir."

The man put the truck slowly through its gears.

The bath had done what it could for Althea. She was warm, but felt full of a strange energy. She dressed, walked onto the boardwalk, and quickly found her way to the fortune-teller's booth. The fortune-teller was haggling with a group of teenagers, and Althea bided her time and watched families shuffle by on the promenade.

When the teenagers filed out, laughing, Althea entered.

"I'll be right with you," the fortune-teller said.

Althea took a seat. The fortune-teller got up and moved behind a curtain into a little, makeshift office. Althea saw her drink from a wine bottle.

"I can come back," Althea said. "I don't even have any real money on me, anyway."

The fortune-teller peered around the curtain. She took another drink and offered the bottle to Althea.

"No, thanks, ma'am."

"People who seek me out only for their *childish* amusement make me very, very angry," the fortune-teller said. Althea nodded.

"What can I do for you?"

"I don't know," Althea said. "I have such negative thoughts in my head."

"Yes," the fortune-teller said. "Negative is a good word to describe one's thoughts."

Althea stood up. "I shouldn't be here," she said. "I don't even have any money."

The fortune-teller motioned for Althea to sit.

"I was just about to do my nightly reading of my crystal ball. You look like a nice girl. You are welcome to stay and bear witness with me."

Althea sat back down. The fortune-teller disappeared fully behind the curtain, and came back with a glass ball and a small wooden stand. She took off her scarf and dragged it over the ball repeatedly. Her hair, red as fire, streamed out from under her headdress.

Althea heard the fortune-teller muttering under her breath. She released the scarf and let it rest on the ball.

"What do you see?" Althea asked.

"Nothing yet."

The fortune-teller raised her arms. Her long fingers flared out and her head tilted back. Althea saw the fortune-teller's eyes darting, and then they rolled back completely into her head.

A breeze came in from the boardwalk, and the scarf twittered, then blew across the small room. The fortune-teller opened her eyes.

"Thank you, *spirits*," she said.

Althea watched the fortune-teller place her eye directly against the curve of the globe. She began, again, to speak under her breath.

"Do you see something now?" Althea asked.

"I do," she said. "In the future. It is not too far off. Six months. Maybe more. It is an *unpleasant* future. A great and evil wind will blow ashore. I see . . . *absolute destruction*."

Suddenly the fortune-teller gasped and sputtered. She stood, reached for the wine bottle, and drank. The bottle emptied, and the fortune-teller placed it down. She gathered her crystal ball and retreated into the closet.

Althea reached down and picked up the scarf. She placed it on the table underneath the wooden stand.

Outside, no one seemed to have noticed the fortune-teller's outburst. People milled about and cued up for rides and games of chance. Althea found the first ramp off the boardwalk and made her way through the streets with great alacrity. Guy would be home by now, she just knew it.

Any worry Guy had that the driver might smell fuel on him had vanished. As they drove along, the smell in the truck's cab only intensified.

"What do you haul?"

"This is heating oil," the man said. "Mostly for businesses. A few private homes."

Guy leaned toward his open window.

"I'm going all over town, son. Where you want to be dropped?"

"You know the Stardust?"

The man laughed. He reached out and tried to adjust his side mirror. "Who don't know the Stardust?"

"That's close enough to where I'm going," Guy said.

The man looked over at Guy. "You know you're bleeding?"

Guy nodded.

"You a psycho?"

"Just got lost in the woods. Friend of mine pulled a prank."

The man pulled a hat off the seat and put it on. "You seen that movie? *Psycho*?"

Guy shook his head.

"Love that Hitchcock. He's got another one out, you know? I don't go to the pictures as much as I'd like to go."

Guy kept breathing the fresh air from outside the cab. "How long now?"

"Not long, son. We're on the Rio Grande."

The man stopped talking, and so did Guy. The breeze whipped through the cab, but the smell of fuel was still sickening. The man didn't even seem to notice it as he pulled off his hat and set it back on the seat. Guy saw that it was a military hat.

"You were in the military?"

"Fought in Africa, in World War II. Would have fought in Korea too, but I was too broken down. I drive this truck just to get off of my ass and away from the missus."

Guy looked at the man's face. He hadn't realized he was so old.

The truck kept lurching along, finding its way through its long series of gears. Guy started to recognize landmarks, and finally, he spotted the Skylark Motel. He couldn't see any light coming from their motel room.

"Here's good."

The driver downshifted and applied the brakes. Guy re-checked his jacket pockets for the money.

"Thanks, sir. Really."

Guy got out and closed the door. It was heavy, and didn't quite latch. The driver reached across the seat and pulled it shut. Guy waved him off and walked through the parking lot toward his room.

Under a lamppost, he took inventory of his cuts. He found a Jeep, reached in, and turned the mirror to his face. The scratches were obvious, but not deep.

As the parking lot lights allowed, he inspected his legs. He looked, he thought, like he had rolled around on a bale of bristled hay. It wasn't the size of the cuts that caused him pain, he realized, but the gnawing sting of the fuel. He smelled his fingers.

The trunk. He must have picked up the fuel when he closed the trunk.

The pool was closed, but he hopped the fence and climbed down the ladder. The water burned his cuts beyond what he had expected. Guy put his hands together underwater and rubbed them. He stood still in the water for a minute, then looked around. Diving below, he held his breath for a few seconds, and reemerged.

Guy walked over to the stairs and exited the pool, and shook off what water he could. His feet felt like concrete as he made his way to the room.

At the door, he patted his pants pockets for the key. Althea opened the door.

Neither of them said a word. They embraced. Althea pulled back first, her hands still around his neck, and her nose wrinkled.

"You're soaking," she said. "And you're *really* here."

"I am," Guy said. "But we have to leave." He pulled her inside and closed the door.

"Close the drapes," he said.

Althea pulled the drapes shut. She started to ask why, but caught sight of Guy's cuts.

"Guy, your *face*."

He went into the bathroom and looked in the mirror. In the full light, he saw that the cuts were just beginning to scab over. He lathered his hands with soap and lightly rubbed his face. Althea came up behind him.

"Why do we have to leave?"

"Something went wrong," Guy said. "And I can't tell you about it."

Althea moved back into the room and sat on the bed. "I had such negative thoughts tonight."

Guy put the two duffel bags on the bed. He unzipped them and began pushing stray clothes into them haphazardly.

"Let me see my makeup bag," Althea said. "Where is it? I have to have something I can put on those cuts."

"The soap is fine."

Guy tossed her shoes next to her on the bed. The first bag was now nearly full, and he secretly pulled the small band of cash out of his jacket and placed it into his pants pocket. He zipped Max's jacket into the duffel bag and turned toward her.

"That's Max's jacket," Althea said.

Guy nodded.

"Did you two have a fight?"

"Kind of," he said. "It's all okay now."

Althea put her shoes on.

"You trust me, Althea?"

"Of course."

A car door slammed outside in the parking lot. Guy pulled back the drapes and looked out.

"Stay here," he said.

Guy made it to the taxicab just before it pulled away. He opened its back door.

"You for hire?"

"That was my last fare," the man said.

Guy pulled out the band of money and peeled off a ten-dollar note.

"How about now?"

The driver reached into the backseat and took the ten.

"Two minutes," Guy said. He went back into the motel room and grabbed the duffel bags.

"I have more things," Althea said.

"Grab them."

Guy went back out to the taxicab with the one full bag. He knocked on the trunk, and the driver came around to meet him.

"You'll be taking us to the Little White Wedding Chapel."

"Got it," the man said.

Althea came out with the last bag. The driver took it from her and put the duffels in the trunk.

"*One minute*," Guy said. He waited for the driver to close the trunk and get back in the cab.

"Althea, will you marry me *tonight*?"

She took a step back. Guy lowered himself to one knee. "*Trust* me," he said.

"Okay," she said. "I do."

The cab driver honked his horn. Guy stood, leaned in to Althea, and kissed her.

"We have to do it now," he said.

She put her arms around him. "Don't let go," she said.

The driver honked again. Guy took Althea's hand and led her into the cab.

The driver wound quickly through the streets. Althea leaned on Guy's shoulder. Her fingers traced the small cuts on his cheek.

"This is as close as I can park," the driver said.

They got out, and Guy pulled the bags from the trunk. "We'll have to wake up Neil."

Althea reached for one of the bags, but Guy kept them both. It was a short, congested walk to the front door of the chapel, and neither of them seemed to notice anything but the path from the cab to the door. When they got there, Guy set the bags down and knocked.

"I don't think he's here," Althea said.

Guy stepped back and looked at Althea. "You put on your wedding dress," he said.

"I did. It's not as I'd hoped."

"I'm sorry. I know you wanted to buy a nice, new one." Guy stepped up to the door and knocked more loudly. "I'll change my clothes inside."

Althea walked to the side of the building. "Maybe try the back door?"

"Good idea."

Althea came back over and sat on the duffel bags. She lifted her dress and let it fall across her legs. She was cold now, and unzipped a duffel bag.

The door opened, and Neil stood in the entrance way. He wore a bathrobe and slippers.

"Althea?"

"Pastor Kleiss."

"I see you are in your wedding dress. What's going on?"

Althea feigned a smile and called out for Guy. Hearing no reply, she turned her attention to Neil. "Guy went around back to look for another door."

Neil turned and looked through the back windows. "I think I see him coming," he said.

Guy emerged from the side of the building.

"Guy. What happened to you?"

Guy grabbed the duffel bags and pushed his way inside. He turned and faced Neil. "It's a long story, Pastor. The short story is we need to get married right now."

"Need to?"

"Right now."

Althea followed Guy inside and Neil joined them.

"I have to change," Neil said. He looked down at Guy's short pants and cut legs.

"Same here, Pastor."

Neil motioned for Guy to follow him into the dressing room. Guy unzipped one duffel bag, and then the other. He found a relatively clean madras shirt and jeans. He held them up to Althea.

"Those will do," she said.

Althea took a seat on a folding chair and waited. She tried to keep her mind on the fact that she was exchanging vows. That was what mattered. They were not strangers in the chapel, and that was important to her. No unwanted guests were there. It was only them and they were what mattered.

Guy came out of the dressing room first. He crossed the room and went through the duffels. He pulled out a drawstring bag.

"What is it?" Althea asked.

Guy crossed the room, smiling, and took a seat next to her.

"Althea," he said, "I've wanted to marry you from the first day I saw you. Remember that day?"

Althea nodded. She had not thought about that day in some time. It came clearly to her as he spoke. "You showed up at my uncle's apple orchard. I took you around to all the best trees. And you kissed me."

"We were just kids."

"We were young," he said. "But I knew I wanted to spend my life with you."

Guy pulled the drawstring. He took Althea's hand and opened it.

"These belonged to my parents," he said. "They loved each other. I'm sure of that."

The rings fell into her hand. One settled atop the other. He closed her hand around the rings.

"I love you truly," he said. He placed his fingers beneath her chin and lifted her face. "Don't cry."

Althea opened her hand and found the smaller ring. She placed it in his palm. "I don't know how I had the nerve to kiss you that day," she said.

They brought their heads together softly.

Neil cleared his throat. They turned and looked at him. He smiled. He was swathed in his official frock, and he held his arms up before them.

"Let us begin," he said.

The ceremony was over as quickly as it began. Neil wished them well, and Guy made a donation to the chapel in exchange for Neil tying up any legal, loose ends.

They were married now, Neil told them. He led them out the door. The couple sat on the bench outside the chapel and looked at one another.

"We have to leave Wildwood. Right now," Guy said.

Althea looked around at the boardwalk, at all it held that they had not experienced. Guy saw tears in her eyes. He figured she was more disappointed to miss out on the planned honeymoon than to have had such a rushed wedding.

"Why don't we go north," he said, "and honeymoon in Atlantic City? It will be just as good there."

Althea put her arms around him. "Let's," she said.

They took up their bags and headed down the ramp. A horn honked twice. Guy saw their cab driver in the distance.

"He waited," Althea said. "Wonderful!"

The driver helped them with their bags. Guy handed him another ten-dollar bill.

"Skylark?"

"No," Guy said. "We need to catch a bus."

They got in the cab and the driver took them to the bus terminal. He looked at them in the rearview mirror repeatedly as he drove. It made Guy nervous.

"Where are you two kids going?"

Althea started to speak, but Guy moved his body in front of hers and spoke loudly. "It's a surprise," he said. He gave Althea a look that he hoped she would follow.

"Right," she said. "He never tells me *anything*."

The driver kept his eyes on the mirror as much as he did the road. When the bus terminal came into view, Guy dropped a few one-dollar bills onto the front seat.

"We'll get the bags inside by ourselves," Guy said.

"You're the boss." The driver opened the trunk and handed them each a bag.

The terminal was nearly empty. Guy waited the minute it took the driver to leave the parking lot before taking Althea inside.

"I'll get the tickets," he said. "You have a seat and watch the bags."

Guy went over to the counter. He told the ticket agent he wanted two tickets to Atlantic City. After he said "two," he looked back and saw Althea sitting on a bench and lifting Max's jacket from the duffel bag.

"No! Althea!"

Guy could see that he had startled her, and a man emptying a nearby trash bin put down the can and stared at him. Guy ran to Althea, arms stretched out to grab the jacket.

"Guy? What?"

"Don't touch that jacket," he said. "It's dirty, and wet." He bent down next to her and grabbed it. “It’s not something you should touch.”

Althea looked down at her wedding dress.

“I forgot I was wearing this,” she said. Guy sat down next to her on the bench.

“Are you cold?”

“Not really,” she said. “Not with you next to me.” She took his hand in hers and traced her fingertip along his ring. “Your ring fits very well.”

“I had it sized. We’ll get your ring sized, too.”

Althea put her hand out in front of them so both she and Guy could look at her ring. It was a little loose, but it stayed in place.

“So shiny,” she said.

“I had them polished. They looked a little like copper when my uncle got them out to give to me, the day I told him we were eloping.”

The ticket agent tapped Guy on the shoulder.

“That Atlantic City bus is about to leave. You want to pay for these two one-way tickets or not?”

Guy paid him, and the ticket agent gave the tickets to Althea. He smiled at her, wished them well, and returned to his station.

The bus was relatively empty, and no one had taken the back. “We can sit back there,” Guy said. “Sprawl out.”

Althea looked at him, then down at the hard, empty seats.

“It’s okay,” he said. “You can sleep up against me back there. I’ll keep you warm.”

On the map in the bus terminal, the ride north had looked much shorter than he had imagined it could be. When he had decided on the elopement plan, Atlantic City seemed a world away from Wildwood, but in reality, it wasn’t. He wondered if Atlantic City would be far enough away to be safe. He watched the lights go by outside the window and absentmindedly stroked Althea’s hair. Each time the bus hit a sizeable bump, Althea asked if they were already there. Guy marveled at the way she seemed asleep and awake at the same time.

Atlantic City was more like a big city than he had imagined. The hotels were larger, taller, and as they began to appear, he tasted the acid rising from his stomach.

Althea felt him moving. “What is it?”

“We’re here,” he said. “That’s all.”

The bus released its air brakes, and Guy and Althea gathered their bags and stepped into the parking lot.

"Over there," he said. "Go get that cab."

Althea jogged slowly toward the cab while Guy struggled along with the two duffel bags.

"Guy, he's free."

The driver was an old man, very old, and his cocked hat reached down into his eyes. He came over and took the bags from Guy. "Where to?"

"What's a good hotel?"

The driver opened the back door, and Althea climbed in. "Couple of young white kids like you? How old 'you? Where you from?"

"We're on our honeymoon," Guy said. "So I guess something nice."

"Oh, okay," the driver said. "Let's see. How 'bout the Traymore?"

Guy stooped down and looked in at Althea. She looked very sleepy. He looked back at the man. "Is the Traymore nice?"

"It's *famous.*"

Guy got in next to Althea and shut the door. The driver took his seat and adjusted the radio.

"You minding my music?"

"It's fine," Guy said.

The cabbie put the taxi into drive. He found some distant jazz on his radio and tapped along in syncopation on the steering wheel. Guy saw the old man's face in the rearview mirror.

"Pretty enough dress your girl got," he said. "Uh-huh."

Althea leaned forward to meet the old man's eyes in the mirror. She smiled at him and put her head back on Guy's shoulder.

"I'm *really* tired," she said.

"Me too."

The driver knew his way around town, and he managed to drive with one foot on the brake and one foot on the gas. Guy realized all cabbies did to some degree. The driver stopped tapping, put his arm across the front seat, and opened his hand.

"Let's make it three for everything," he said.

Guy gave him the money. Then he peeled off two more dollars and offered them.

"You go on and keep that," the driver said. "You young and you married now." He pulled up to the Traymore Hotel, just off the boardwalk entrance. "Okay?"

Guy nodded. The driver pulled their bags from the trunk. Guy tried to help him, but the old man yanked them free and dropped them onto the ground.

The couple watched the cab pull away, and together they stood and took in what they could see of the enormous Traymore Hotel. Althea kissed Guy on the cheek, and ran and skipped off toward the front entrance. She quickly felt a pang, a lack of energy, and she stopped running and walked. She had been running too much, and not sleeping, she knew, and now wanted nothing more than a warm bed.

Althea entered the lobby and plopped down on a settee. When Guy found her, after checking them in, she was practically asleep.

A young bellhop helped them with their bags and took the couple up in the elevator to their room on the third floor. He opened the door and Guy gave him a dollar for his troubles. The bellhop stowed the dollar and carried the bags into the room.

"This hotel was opened as a boarding house," he said.

Althea fell onto the bed. She stretched her arms.

"'Round eighteen-hundred, maybe eighteen-ten," the bellhop said.

Guy pulled out another dollar and held open the door. The bellhop came back to take the money. He doffed his cap at Guy and left.

Room service knocked on the door. Guy rubbed at his eyes. There was just enough light through the open drape to expose Althea sleeping on the bed.

"I'm opening the door," he said.

Guy stood in the doorway, signed the bill, and pulled the food cart inside.

Althea, dressed in her underwear, emerged from the covers and walked gracefully to the cart. "This smells *so* good," she said.

Guy dragged two chairs into position. The couple sat next to the cart and fed one another eggs and bacon. Althea smeared copious amounts of marmalade on her toast and licked it off.

"How long will we *honeymoon*?" she asked.

Guy took some of his orange juice down the wrong pipe.

"I don't know." He coughed. "Forever?"

"Yes," she said. "Can we afford it?"

Guy looked around. The wallpaper was outdated, but the room was oversized for two: Besides the large bed, the room housed four chairs, a sideboard, and two small tables. The bathroom was as large as their whole main rooms had been at the smaller motels.

"I took this room on the third floor to save money. If we were ten floors up, with a great beach view, then *no* on the forever."

Althea smiled and went to the window. She pulled the drape aside.

"It's not a *bad* view, here," she said.

Guy nodded.

"I can *kind* of see the water. You know?"

"Good," he said. "I told the front desk you'd like it, even if it's a partial view."

Althea turned and looked at Guy.

"Is that what they call it? Partial view?" She came over and sat on the edge of the bed. "Partial view doesn't sound too romantic, though. Does it?"

"No," he said. "I guess it sounds kind of so-so."

Althea came back to the cart and finished her orange juice. Then she said, "I'm still thirsty. You want a glass of water from the bathroom tap?"

Guy offered her the rest of his orange juice instead. "I'd check that tap water for sea salt before you ever drink it."

Althea drank Guy's orange juice and wiped the back of her hand across her mouth. "Is that true? Is the water from the tap actually salty?"

Guy put all the dishes on the cart and pushed it into the hall. He came back in and sat down on the bed. "I've heard that about the tap water in Atlantic City, that it used to be salty up here. Who told me that? I can't remember."

Guy thought about Max. It was Max who had told him that, and Guy almost said so.

"Maybe it was in the spigots for saltwater baths," Althea said. "Like when I was at the hot springs down in Arkansas."

Guy lay down and looked up at her. "You went to Hot Springs, Arkansas?"

"I never told you that?"

Guy shook his head.

"I was really little. My dad took us with him on one of his business trips. My mom loved soaking in those hot springs. We did it all day, every day." Althea brushed at her hair with her fingers.

"Did you—you know. Go to the rallies?"

Althea sat down next to Guy on the bed.

"No, Guy. I didn't. I told you, my mom and I went to the springs."

Althea left the bed quickly. She crossed the room and stopped at the window.

"I'm not my father," she said.

Guy joined her at the window. They watched the bathers making their way across the boardwalk to the beach.

"I'm going to take a shower," he said.

Althea waited at the window until she heard the water running. She got undressed, put on her bathing suit, and descended the stairs.

The Traymore's lobby seemed musty and too ornate to Althea. Something about the whole place reminded her of decay. Outside on the boardwalk, Althea found that the ocean was close enough to smell, and she stopped and took in the salty air. The tall buildings seemed to hover and lean over the boardwalk.

The Traymore Hotel truly was a monstrous building, and in the daylight its Gothic appeal felt subdued. Still, the closeness of the water meant she could swim and still make it back, before Guy had a chance to wonder where she went.

The water was cold. Althea's experience with ocean water was almost entirely from the Gulf of Mexico, and from the warm southern-infused waters of Virginia Beach. She waded in enough to get the ocean's full effect. After a minute she had already had enough, and quickly retreated up the boardwalk stairs. A bench opened up, and she wrapped her arms around herself and shook her legs heartily to create warmth.

"Althea!"

She could hear Guy's voice, but from where she sat, she couldn't see him. This boardwalk was wider than Wildwood's, and abundantly more crowded.

"Althea. *There* you are." Guy emerged from the crowd and sat down next to her on the bench. "You don't have a towel," he said. He pulled his fingers across his short hair, and she saw it was still wet from his shower.

"You've had a dip in the ocean," he said. She nodded. Guy put his arm across the back of the bench.

"This is nice," he said.

"It is. Let me just get a towel, Guy, and I'll be back."

No one batted an eye as she dripped her way across the Traymore's lobby. She took the elevator and got off on the highest floor she could reach. The window next to the elevator was tall, and she looked through it toward the beach. She tried to look for Guy, but there were so many benches along the boardwalk that she couldn't be sure which was his.

The elevator doors opened. A family got out, and the young daughter pointed at Althea. "Don't point at strangers," the mother said. "It isn't nice."

Althea smiled and managed to catch the elevator door before it closed. She rode down to the third floor and found Guy standing outside their room.

"Why don't you change, and we'll go out?"

"Okay," she said. "Where to?"

It didn't take too long for them to reach the end of the boardwalk, by way of a rolling chair. Guy tipped the tired, chair operator. He took Althea by the hand and led her down to the beach.

"Do you think it's beautiful here?" he asked.

"I do," she said. She looked at the azure sky. "Do I look beautiful?"

"Of course."

They walked on and took in the air. The couple noticed many children as they neared the edge of Atlantic City. They watched them throw balls, build castles in the sand, and frolic in the shallow pools of water. On the couple's other side, the boardwalk was busy with the rolling click of the chairs across the planks. Shopkeepers were opening their food stands and shouting for men to engage in games of chance.

They took a ramp up to the boardwalk, and Althea pulled off her shoes and socks. With her free hand, she swatted at the sand.

"What do you want to do?"

"I don't know," she said. She put her shoes and socks back on, then spotted the fortune-teller's sign.

"There," she said. "Remember how I said we should go and see a fortune-teller?"

"Really?"

"It seems like something people do for fun on boardwalks, Guy. You'll love it!"

Althea brushed her way past several strolling people as she crossed the boardwalk. Guy barely managed to keep up with her.

"I don't see it," he said.

Althea extended her arm and pointed. "Wow," he said. "You saw that sign from back there?"

She took him by the wrist and dragged him toward the booth.

The parlor was bigger than the one she visited in Wildwood. The woman inside was much older. As the couple entered, she said, "Have a seat."

The old woman readied her tarot cards on the table. Guy looked at Althea. He could see she loved the idea of such fantasy.

Guy leaned in and whispered to Althea, "She's not an *actual* Gypsy."

"I know that. But look at her face. Isn't she interesting-looking?"

"I heard that," the old woman said. "And I am *most* interesting to look at. I've sailed every sea, crossed every mountain pass. I've seen things that don't even exist!"

Althea placed her palms out and extended her arms.

"I don't believe this," Guy said.

The old woman took Althea's hands in hers. She smiled at Althea and then smirked at Guy. Althea laughed. Guy sat back and looked around at the walls. There was not a single placard to suggest who the woman was, or whether she had anything beyond a peddler's license. He started to ask the old woman her name, but Althea turned and shushed him.

"You have a good heart line," the old woman said. She looked at Guy as she said it. Then she traced Althea's palm with her forefinger. The old woman closed her eyes and folded Althea's hand.

"I sense something, someone, haunting you."

Althea looked at Guy. He rolled his eyes at her.

"Do you believe in the *spirit* world?" The old woman rose as she spoke, and opened her eyes wide.

"Come on," Guy said.

He stood, and grabbed at Althea's free hand.

The old woman sat down with an exasperated sigh. She released Althea's hand.

"You, sir, have broken the *spiritual vine*. I can no longer see the presence clearly."

She held her hand out and subtly rubbed her fingers together. Guy took two ones out of his wallet and paid her.

"Who was it?" Althea asked.

The old woman looked at the two one-dollar bills, and then at Guy. "Likely a ghost," she said.

Guy yanked Althea over to the door.

"Next time," the old woman said, "we will read your cards."

Guy raised his hand and extended his middle finger. Althea apologized for him and pushed him along.

By the time they arrived at the Ritz-Carlton, Guy had given in to Althea's ghost fears. The line at the front desk was long, and the couple spent their time in silence. When the desk clerk finally asked how he could help them, Althea gave Guy a final nudge with an elbow in his back.

"Checking in," Guy said.

The clerk pushed a form toward Guy. "Type of room you request?"

"Something high up," Althea said.

"She wants a clear view of the ocean," Guy said.

The clerk smiled now, and checked his ledger. "How long will you be staying with us?"

Guy finished filling out the form. "Until our honeymoon is over," Althea said.

The clerk kept up his smile and made a notation. "How many bags?"

Althea stared at Guy.

"*I'm* not going back to that *haunted* hotel," she said.

"There's really no *ghost* there," Guy said.

The clerk gaped, and then rubbed his hands together like a hungry child. "There's a haunted hotel here in our city? Which one? Do tell."

Guy gave them both a look.

"Can you have someone go and get the bags?" Althea asked.

The clerk snapped his fingers, and a bellhop appeared.

"They're at the Traymore," Guy said. The clerk wrote it down on a piece of paper, and the bellhop went on his way.

"I should have guessed," the clerk said. "*The Traymore.*"

"It's creepy, isn't it?" Althea said.

The clerk pretended to shiver. He handed the room key to Guy.

"I assume getting those bags, *that* will cost me?"

The clerk laughed at him, and motioned for the next person in line.

Althea took Guy's hand and led him to the restaurant off the lobby. The sign said that the special of the day was lobster bisque. They took a seat and ordered two. When they finished the bisque, they ate an extra basket of bread between them.

Guy finished and pushed back his chair. "They may be back with the bags by now. Do you want to go see your new room?"

"No. I want to do something *fun*," Althea said.

Outside, they walked for a block or so, and then hired a rolling chair. They passed by shops and hotels and restaurants, and soon they were near the Traymore.

"Do you think they got our bags, Guy?"

"Sure," he said. "Of course, we could go in and ask, if you like."

She knew he was teasing her about the ghost.

When they spotted a crowd they stopped the chair and got out. The man was tired, Guy could see, and he paid him double the rate.

"What is it?" Althea asked.

They pushed their way slowly through the crowd. Guy looked over the shoulders of those he could.

"It's Ripley's," he said. "It's the freak show place."

They cut and weaved and finally broke into the open. The crowd kept a polite distance from the attraction, and the couple stared at two men in matching white rocking chairs. The men seemed to be fused to the rockers. The promotional sign in front read, "Fattest Twins in the World."

"This is an ugly spectacle," Althea said.

A man in a straw hat broke in. "I've seen fatter people," he said, "but never fatter twins."

Althea looked around at the crowd. Then she looked back at the twins. "Do they just sit there?"

"I think so," Guy said.

Althea shook her head.

"We're the freaks," she said. "We're supposed to stand here and stare at them?"

Guy pulled her along behind him and they made their way out of the crowd. He walked them past Central Pier and over to the railing on the beach side.

"I feel a little faint," Althea said.

Guy used his hips to push his way onto a crowded bench, then got up and sat Althea down in the space he had made. "You're probably a little hungry. That bisque was pretty light."

Althea pushed on her stomach. "I guess. I'm not sure."

Guy looked around at the storefronts. "I have an idea," he said.

He pulled her to her feet, and kept his arm around her. They cut across the promenade and went inside Fralinger's Candy.

"I'll just sit," Althea said.

She took a seat on the window box. Guy went to the counter and ordered a bag of molasses taffy. He paid, then unwrapped a piece and offered it to her.

"You try it," she said. "I don't think I like the smell."

Guy placed the piece in his mouth. Althea got up and left the store. Guy pocketed the candies, and the couple walked on, slowly, toward Steel Pier.

A man wearing an advertising board walked by and handed Guy a flyer. He read it, then showed it to Althea. It showcased an entertainment act called "The Diving Horse." The man was placing flyers in everyone's hands, and soon the tourists formed a herd and began to stampede toward the attraction.

"You *do* want to see it, *right*?"

Althea shook her head. "That sounds sort of cruel," she said.

"If it was cruel," he said, "they wouldn't be passing flyers out to families." He pointed at all the kids who were racing toward the horse.

Althea stayed with Guy as best she could as he darted toward the front of the growing crowd. "We have to get closer," he said. He took a hold of her wrist and pulled her along. "There's the ramp," he said. "Can you see it?"

Althea lifted her head and looked into the distance. "A little."

They moved a bit to the side of the throng of people so that Althea could see the horse. Clearly visible, the whitewashed wooden ramp stretched four stories into the sky.

A gasp arose from the crowd. They could see the horse now, a beautiful, pure white horse with a pretty young woman astride its back.

"The horse doesn't want to climb," Althea said.

Guy stood on his tiptoes. He could just make out the pool on the other side of the ramp. "He's going to jump into a pool," he said.

Althea turned away. "I don't want to watch."

"I'll tell you what's happening," Guy said.

A man standing next to Althea spoke up. "That gelding loves to do this, honey. It's nothing to fret about." The man took his hat off and waved it about. "Take the dive."

The horse had reached the platform. The young woman blew kisses to the crowd with one hand. She used the other to stroke the horse beneath her.

"It's going to dive," Guy said. "Look!"

"Why doesn't it back up? Why doesn't it turn around?"

"Animals don't like to do that," Guy said. "They like to move *through* openings."

The crowd cheered loudly. The man next to Althea leaned and whispered something in her ear.

Guy glared. "What did he say to you?"

"He said, 'Don't worry, little honey; they get the horse drunk beforehand.'"

Althea pushed the man with the hat out of the way. Guy followed her. Halfway to the back of the crowd, they heard the culling voice of the mob, and the large splash that soon accompanied it. Althea doubled over and emptied the contents of her stomach as the crowd scattered to avoid her.

The room they had secured at the Ritz was a fine one. Guy stared at the ocean through the view that the room's high floor afforded. The bellhop had placed their duffel bags on the bed, and now Althea napped beside them.

Guy accounted for all his money, then decided to unpack the bags.

After, he went down and bought flowers and a vase from the lobby gift shop. The room looked good, and the smell of the flowers, he hoped, would soothe Althea.

The woman had sold him lavender, and instructed him to rub the flowers across the pillow Althea slept on to help her with the vomiting. He was subtle as he did so, but Althea awoke, and he returned the flowers to the vase on the sideboard.

"Did you want me to call room service? Something for your stomach? Some juice?"

Althea didn't speak for a moment. Guy could tell what she really wanted was *nothing*.

"I'm sure it was the lobster that made you sick, but I never get sick, you know. My uncle never cooked food too well, so I think I'm just used to it."

Althea opened her eyes and moved her head enough to see the breadth of the room. Guy opened the drape a little more.

"Those flowers are nice," she said.

"They're supposed to help you feel better. Are you feeling better?"

She shook her head, then nodded.

"Do you want me to leave you to sleep?"

"No," she said. "Stay with me."

"Okay. Do you want to watch television? Listen to the radio?"

Althea sat up a bit. Guy took the pillow from his side of the bed and placed it behind her head.

"Let's just talk," she said.

"About the honeymoon, or what?"

"Sure," she said. She pulled the sheet up around her. "I assumed things I shouldn't have."

Guy moved the bags and sat next to her. "Like what?"

She looked around the room. The walls were replete with wainscoting. The crown molding matched the patterns on the backs of the chairs.

"Like *this*," she said.

Guy touched his hand to her face. She felt a normal temperature to him. "You mean you assumed things because you were . . . rich."

Althea nodded. Guy crossed his legs and stared at his shoes.

"Go on," he said. "What else did you imagine?"

Althea thought for a minute. She knew she wanted to be honest. "Well . . . I saw all those pictures in the magazines of the Kennedy wedding."

"We *all* saw those," Guy said.

She touched his hair with the tips of her fingers. "I know. I mean I really lost myself in those photos. And the Kennedy homes in Georgetown. I just fell in love with them."

"That was pretty close to the year we met," he said. "Their wedding."

Althea smiled.

"You know, my uncle saw him once," Guy said. "He was making a delivery, apples and things, to Georgetown University, and he saw Jack Kennedy jog by."

"You told me that," she said. Guy nodded.

"But what do *you* want?" he said. "I mean, we're not the Kennedys. But what?"

Althea ran her hands through her hair and scratched at her scalp. She felt blindsided by the question. "No one's ever really asked me that before."

"Take your time."

"A *trousseau*."

"A what?"

"Bridal clothing. For the honeymoon."

Guy lay back. Without his pillow behind him, he stared straight at the ceiling.

"Like the dresses your father burned, you mean. Like that?"

Althea leaned over him. Her long hair fell across his face. "Kind of," she said. "With a color scheme. Like Jackie's Chanels."

She sat up, then stood and walked over to the sideboard and picked out a flower.

"You'd still have those pretty dresses of yours," Guy said, "if you had married someone from your kind."

Althea smelled the flower, and then put it back in the vase.

"I don't know if he really *burned* them. He just didn't want me dating you and figured if he took my nice things away . . . "

"You're just a rich Protestant and I'm just a poor Catholic," he said. "It is what it is."

"I'm not an anything," she said. "I don't think I even believe in God."

Guy sat up. He stared at her. "Don't say that, Althea."

Althea started to say something else, but stopped herself. She crossed to the window.

"Jackie wore a *fawn* coat at the inauguration. Jeannie taught me that word."

"I don't want to talk about Jeannie and Max."

Althea turned to face him. "You want to know *what* I want?"

Guy nodded.

"An engagement ring."

Guy sighed.

"I'm not a spoiled rich girl, Guy, just because I want a diamond ring."

"I never said you were."

The knock on the door froze them both. Guy answered it. He stepped into the hall and a man told him to come and pay his bill.

Guy stuck his head back into the room. "I have to go settle the hotel bill," he said. Althea said nothing, and he shut the door behind him.

The man Guy followed down the hall wore a smart suit, and as they entered the elevator, he produced an operating key. The man worked the elevator and brought up his coat at the side, revealing not his identification, but his holstered gun.

"Are you with the police?"

The man shook his head, and turned the key again. The elevator doors opened. "Down at the end of the hall," he said.

Guy got out and walked slowly through the corridor. He paused for a moment to consider what might happen to him. He looked around for an exit, or a stairwell entrance.

"Keep going."

The hall led to a single large door and a large man sitting in a too-small chair. The man jumped to his feet more quickly than Guy had imagined possible.

"Spread."

Guy didn't move. The large man swung him around and pinned him to the wall, his elbow in Guy's back.

"If you're carrying, tell me now."

Guy's eyes opened wide, and he fought to spit out his words. "A gun?"

"Or a knife or anything else."

The large man finished his pat-down and opened the door to reveal a penthouse apartment. He sat back down in his chair.

Guy entered the room slowly. All the drapes were closed, and he saw that the apartment ran the entire length of the building. A lamp in the center of the main room drew a bluish smoke into its lamp shade.

"Sit," a voice said.

Guy came around the chair to find himself looking at a man seated in an oversized leather chair.

"Sit."

Guy sat across from the man.

"Sam?"

"Good to see you again, Guy." Sam offered Guy a cigar.

"What are you doing here, sir?"

Sam laughed. He had the kind of laugh, Guy thought, that made you feel happy, and a little nervous at the same time. "I think I might ask you that same question, Guy. Yes?"

Guy nodded.

"I suppose, after certain events transpired, that you thought, perhaps, you might abstain from seeing any former downstate acquaintances?"

Guy did not speak. He looked around the apartment. No one else was there.

"Have I missed the mark?"

"No, sir."

Sam rested his hands across his lap and entwined his fingers. He wore a large cream-colored ring that matched his suit. Guy thought about the suited man outside in the hall, and the one in the elevator.

"The man who brought me here said I had a bill to settle."

Sam waved toward the door. "Don't mind my goons," he said. "A necessary evil of the trade." He picked up his cigar and puffed at it. "Let's get to the nature of the business at hand."

Guy sat as far back in his chair as he could.

"You *do owe* a bill, Guy."

Guy nodded. He swallowed, and heard his throat contract.

"It would seem I have lost a valuable asset in Max. Yes?"

Guy looked at the floor.

"I believe, young Guy, that you are just the person to fill the void. Max spoke very highly of you."

Guy looked directly at Sam. "He did?"

Sam put out the cigar in the ashtray and blew his smoke. "However. There's *always* a however, I'm afraid. Max tells me you neither picked him up at the exit, *nor* went along for the, shall we say, *final ride*."

Guy looked back at the door. He thought he heard someone entering the apartment.

"I have bigger plans for you than Wildwood. And it wouldn't be prudent to place you back in the belly of the whale, now, would it?"

Sam went to the sideboard and retrieved a bottle of scotch and two glasses. "Single malt. Pour you one?"

Guy shook his head.

"Besides which, our mutual, imprisoned friend Max thinks you've gone back to your farm in Virginia. Personally, I don't think we want to test his loyalties by having you shit on his back lawn."

Sam left the drinking paraphernalia on the sideboard and walked behind Guy's chair. He gripped Guy's shoulders and gave them a hard squeeze. Guy sank down in his chair to lessen the grip.

"I need a man I can trust, or at least one indebted to me, to do some intelligent exploration. I'm growing disinterested in Atlantic City, and the truth is, the place is showing its age. There is a thin line between decadence and decay. There is, in my opinion, no *order* here anymore. Little thieves are popping up everywhere, and everyone is falling in love with the torch." Guy knew he was talking about Max.

"I need you, Guy, to be my Lewis and Clark. You will go up to Maine. Ever been?"

Guy shook his head.

"Beautiful place. Untapped place. You will go and travel—your Althea will love it. You will live like the King and Queen. Beaches. Open land. Mountains rising right out of the water."

Sam pulled his hands off Guy and laughed. He came around and resumed his place in the leather chair.

"You will ask around at the hotels. People you meet playing cards. I will supply you everything you need. I have a few contacts that can lead you in the right directions."

Guy sat up in his chair and gathered himself. "Why me? I don't have any knowledge of . . . *anything*."

Sam laughed. He reached over and gave Guy a slap on the knee.

"You have no reason, then, for anyone to suspect your questions to be anything more than naïve. Yes?"

"Questions about what?"

"Numbers. Lotteries. Gambling, my boy. And, eventually, a little loan on the streets, here and there. See how organized, or *unorganized* things are up there in Maine."

Guy felt the blood leave his face.

"Messersmith. Is that British?"

"British, or Irish, I think. Some Welsh. Not sure about the rest."

Sam stood. "Good, good. You do not look ethnic, and that is on our side."

Sam snapped his fingers like a hammer on a nail, and the large man stepped into the room.

"We will speak again, Guy."

The large man came halfway over. Sam extended his hand, and Guy took it.

When Althea turned off the shower, she noticed the blood. The streaks ran the length of her legs, and there was just enough to cover the drain with a light film. She wrapped a towel around herself and opened the bathroom door.

"Guy? Are you back? Guy?"

She took a seat at the desk and dialed the phone. The operator picked up immediately.

"I think I need a doctor," Althea said.

"Is it an emergency?"

Althea opened the towel. The blood had mostly been absorbed. "I don't think so. Maybe a little."

"We have a house doctor. I can put in a call right now."

"How long?" Althea twirled the cord.

"He's on premises right now. I'll have him contacted. Let's see. Hold on."

Althea looked at the blood on the towel. It made her a little nauseous.

"Ma'am? He's right below you. I'll have a bellhop give him the message to come by your room next."

Althea hung up the phone. She realized she hadn't said thank you and picked it back up.

"Hello? Hello? Operator?"

She placed the receiver back on the hook, grabbed her clothes, and got dressed. She pulled her hair up and quickly tied it with a ribbon.

Inside, the bathroom floor was covered with droplets. She used a washcloth, and swabbed a few of them under her foot.

The knock came suddenly.

"Doctor."

"Coming," she said.

Althea took a deep breath and opened the door. The doctor was a frail, older man, and he seemed in a hurry to enter the room and set down his heavy bag.

"I have a lot of patients to see today," he said.

He placed the bag on the bed and opened it. He motioned for Althea to sit. The bed was the closest place, and she took a seat next to his bag. Right away she felt she was showing poor decorum. She blushed and took a seat on the desk chair.

"And what is the problem today, young lady?"

"I had some odd bleeding, down there. In the shower."

The old doctor took out his stethoscope. He listened to her heart.

"And what else?"

"I'm feeling a little different than usual. Nauseous, I guess."

The old doctor took her wrist. He looked at his watch and timed her pulse.

"Food. It smells strongly? Appetite irregular?"

Althea nodded.

"And you have missed your time of the month?"

"Yes," she said.

"I see." He put his stethoscope back in his bag. "How far past?"

"A few weeks."

He took out his light and measured her pupil reactions. He looked down at her left hand.

"You are looking to take care of the pregnancy?"

Althea pushed herself out of the chair and went to the window.

"I'm really pregnant then?"

The doctor put his light back into his bag. "What did you expect?"

"It was only that one time," she said.

The old doctor stared at her.

"I can give you the name of a person who can take care of it, if that's what you want."

The old doctor secured his bag and went to the door.

"How am I pregnant if I'm *bleeding*?"

"Young lady," he said, "you are simply spotting."

Althea stumbled toward the bed and fell onto it. She placed her hand across her forehead. The old doctor struggled over and placed his heavy bag back down beside her. He opened it.

"You are feeling nauseous right now? It's bad?"

Althea nodded.

The old doctor went through his bag and produced a small container of pills. He took out his pen and wrote instructions on the label.

"You take these for the nausea. Are you sleeping well?"

Althea did not move. She tried to breathe slowly. The doctor walked around the bed and picked up a glass of water.

"Here," he said. He opened the container and handed her a dose of the medicine. She took it. "Drink some water."

Althea tilted the glass and drank.

"What is it?"

"It's thalidomide. It will help with the nausea, and help you sleep."

Althea finished the water and handed him the glass. "Shouldn't I get a test? To make sure I'm pregnant?"

The doctor closed his bag. "No need," he said. "Of course, if you do, there's a new method where they inject a frog. They don't even have to kill it. And the larger hospitals, of course, have a test now. No animal involved, but, a lot of cost I assume you don't want to pay." He looked around the room.

Althea felt the pill making her sleepy.

"Like I said, though, there's really no need. I've been a doctor for some forty years. I know a pregnancy when I see one." He went to the door and opened it. "Started out as a medic in the American Expeditionary Force, with General Pershing. Heard of the Argonne Forest?"

Althea tried to shake her head. The old doctor left the room, and the door latched behind him.

Guy came back into the room. Althea was nowhere to be found. He went into the bathroom to look for her. A bloodied washcloth lay on the floor. He stepped back and bumped the doorjamb.

"Althea?"

A low muttering sound came from inside the room. He moved toward the bed and caught a glimpse of Althea's elbow poking out from beneath the sheets.

"Althea?"

He saw no sign of blood on the bedding. Althea breathed steadily.

"Can you hear me?"

He looked around. On the night stand he found a container of pills. He picked it up and read the label, then put his hands on Althea's shoulders and shook her. He heard her muttering.

"Can you hear me?"

Althea opened her eyes halfway.

"Guy. I'm sleeping." Her voice was low, but he heard her clearly.

"You're okay?"

"Mm-hmm."

Guy pulled the covers up and adjusted her pillow. He watched Althea fall back asleep, and listened to her breathe. Then he left the room and went to the lobby. A bellhop brushed past, and Guy had to raise his voice.

"Is there a Catholic church near here?"

The bellhop shrugged and kept walking.

Guy found a cab outside the hotel's street-side entrance. He leaned down and spoke through the passenger side window.

"Take me to the closest Catholic church."

The driver barely had to drive away from the boardwalk. When they stopped at the entrance to the church, he asked if he should wait for Guy.

"No," Guy said. "I can walk back."

Guy paid the cab driver for his trouble and went inside the old, decaying church. He doubted that it was normal confession time, but he went into the booth and waited. The panel immediately slid open. A man's voice, a little high-pitched, spoke. "You mean to confess?"

"I do, Father."

"As you are ready."

Guy took a deep breath and exhaled.

"Forgive me Father, for I have *greatly* sinned."

"What is the nature of your sin?"

Guy stole a glance through the cutout in the ornate panel. The priest looked very young.

"My wife is pregnant," Guy said.

"I think that is cause for rejoicing, not cause for confession."

"My wife, my . . . we had . . . "

"Go on."

"We had sex before our marriage."

"I see."

"It was Mother's Day. We've both lost our mothers. It was . . . the day was my fault. I was weak. It was only the one time. And that must have been it. That had to be the cause of the pregnancy."

"I understand. But now you are married to this woman?"

Guy moved his head close to the wall. He wanted to keep his face from the sight of the priest. "We are married, yes."

"God will not punish your child. It was God that brought you to the altar, and it is God that will bless your union and your child."

"He is punishing me, Father."

The priest cleared his throat. "You feel a child is a punishment? From God?"

"No, Father. But I have sinned in other ways."

The priest's voice deepened. "If you are to confess, in God's House, you must be forthcoming."

Guy nodded. "Yes. Father. I also have done other things I should not have done."

The priest remained silent.

"I have committed crimes."

"I see."

Guy felt his left hand shake. He looked down and rubbed at his wedding ring. "I drove a man's car as a lookout, while he started a fire. A building fire."

"Did you set the fire?"

Guy moved his head away from the partition. "No."

"Did anyone die? Was anyone burned?"

"No, Father. There wasn't really even a fire."

The priest spoke to himself in Latin. Guy could not follow it.

"I want you to say five Hail Marys."

"That's all?"

"God will forgive you."

"That's not enough, Father."

The priest got close to the partition. His voice became quiet. "Was the building a church?"

"No, Father."

"Five Hail Marys."

Guy put his head down. "And I stole money."

"Five Lord's Prayers, additional."

"How can that be enough?"

The priest tapped on the partition with his ring. Guy looked at him through the pattern. "Did you steal from a church?"

Guy shook his head.

"Then these *sins* are not *mortal.*"

"Yes, Father."

The priest spoke again in Latin.

"These prayers will not redeem me, Father."

"In the eyes of God, they will."

"Not in my eyes. Not in my family's eyes."

"You are speaking of looking outside your relationship to God. Are you looking away from God's Church for absolution beyond His Almighty Power?"

Guy stood.

"Be careful of what you are saying, my son."

Guy started to answer. The priest spoke to him in Latin. Guy pulled back the curtain and fled into the church's parking lot. He ran. The Ritz was near enough, but he ran instead to the jewelry store, never stopping or slowing down.

The bell on the door rang out, and Guy made his way to the counter.

He put his arms behind his head to help catch his breath.

"May I *help you*?"

Guy looked at the salesman, took a few more panting breaths, and stepped back from the counter. The jewelry store was small, and each case held only one form of jewelry.

"Where are your engagement rings?" Guy asked.

The man led Guy down the row.

"Here you are, sir." The man tapped on the glass at a selection of tiny diamond rings. He lifted his face and smiled as he did so.

"I don't want these," Guy said loudly. "I came in to see a big ring. The kind they talk about in the old movies."

The salesman looked Guy over head to foot, then turned up the corner of his mouth. It was obvious that he was trying to draw attention to Guy's clothes with his eyes. Guy looked down at his worn jeans, then back at the man, who was neatly dressed in pinstripes and wearing a diamond tiepin.

"Are you a *jeweler*?"

"I am a jewelry *salesman*."

Guy pulled out his wallet and removed a wad of cash. He slapped the money onto the counter. "Then sell me a *diamond*. Salesman."

The salesman raised his eyebrows and stared at the money.

"Cash? How *lovely*," he said.

He immediately went to retrieve the keys for the case. He picked up the keys, returned, and pulled a one-carat ring out of the case. He placed the ring on a runner of black velvet.

Guy pulled the money off the counter and replaced it in his wallet.

"I have an even lovelier cut for you, sir. Let me get it out. One and a half carats," the salesman said.

Guy looked at the one-carat ring again. He placed his hand against his wallet.

"No, thanks," Guy said. "I don't do business with crooks like you."

The salesman harrumphed, and Guy turned and angrily opened the door. The bell pealed, and Guy pulled and pushed at the door as the bell's noise became almost deafening.

He walked slowly back to the lobby of the Ritz. No one was at the front desk. He spotted a small silver bell and slapped at it until a woman hurriedly emerged from the back office.

"May I help you?"

"You may," Guy said. "I need to settle the bill for retrieving my bags from the Traymore. Two bags."

The woman looked through her ledger.

"Yes. Okay. Name?"

"Messersmith. Guy."

The woman flipped the pages. She found her mark, and then flipped to another page in the ledger.

"You appear to have a bill coming from the doctor that saw—is it your wife?"

Guy looked down at the ledger. He couldn't read the small writing. "How much was that?"

"I don't know," she said. "Doctors bill on their own. Let me see."

She looked in the area above the key-hold, then in the room's mail slot. She pulled out a piece of paper and read it, then slid the paper back into the mail slot.

"He hasn't submitted the bill to your room yet, it would seem."

"Fine. How much for the bag pickup?"

"Covered," she said. "Compliments of the Ritz."

Guy put his wallet back in his pocket. "Listen," he said, "are you folks hiring?"

The woman pointed across the lobby. "In there," she said. "The café needs busboys for the summer."

Guy turned and looked. "Is that the only place?"

The woman nodded. "I can call the café manager and see if he can talk to you."

"I'll sit over there."

Guy took a seat on a velvet couch near the hotel's boardwalk entrance. The manager came out before Guy even got comfortable.

"You want to bus tables in my café?"

The man extended his hand, and Guy shook it. The man smelled like grease.

"Do busboys make any tips?"

"Sure, in a way. The waiters tip the busboys at the end of their shifts." The man took a pen from behind his ear, and a small pad from his pocket. "Name?"

"Guy Messersmith."

"Got it. You start tomorrow." Guy watched him stow the pen.

"Just like that?"

"It isn't exactly a glamorous job, Guy. It's more about whether you want to work hard and earn a day's pay than how skilled you are."

Guy nodded.

"Five in the morning. We'll get you settled in then."

They shook on it, and Guy watched the manager go back into the café. He took the elevator to their room and found Althea awake, but groggy.

"I'm feeling better," she said.

"The medicine." Guy went over to the night stand, picked up the bottle, and read, "'Take for nausea from pregnancy.'" He smiled at her.

"I'm glad that you're pregnant," he said.

"You are?"

Guy sat on the bed and stroked her bangs. "It didn't happen the way it should have. But I'm okay with it happening."

She nodded, and smiled. "I thought you would hate me," she said.

"No," he said. "I want to be a good father. I want to be a man. I'm like a boy, and I want to be a man."

Althea laughed. "Like the play. Like Biff Lowman."

Guy shrugged.

"In *Death of a Salesman*," she said.

"I don't know."

Althea sat up. "I can't remember if he says it in the play I read, or in the play I saw."

Guy pulled the cover completely away from her body. He placed his hand on her stomach and rubbed a circle. "We're going to have a little boy."

"Little girl," she said. She rubbed her stomach with him. "I'm feeling much better now."

He leaned in and kissed her. "I got a job."

Althea smiled. She put her head against his. "Doing what?"

"Busboy. At the café downstairs."

"Good," she said. "I like it here at the Ritz."

Guy stood up. He put his hand on his wallet absentmindedly. "I won't be able to afford staying here."

"We'll get a place of our own," she said. "When the honeymoon is over."

Guy walked over to the window and put his forehead against it. He watched the people below enjoying the evening along the promenade. "And I won't be able to buy you an engagement ring."

Althea got up and walked behind him. She put her hands across his chest.

"We're *already* married," she said.

In the morning there was a soft rap on the door. The room was still pitch-black, and Guy tripped over a shoe on his way to halt the knocking. He opened the door and a man with 'Reggie' printed on his name tag stood there, pointing and tapping at his watch.

"Mister, you're supposed to be at the café."

"The manager sent you? How'd he know I was here?"

Reggie shrugged, and tapped at his watch again.

"Two minutes," Guy said.

Guy dressed in the dark. He shaved without shaving cream, and quickly used the toilet. When he arrived downstairs, the café was already busy.

Reggie set him up with an apron, and told him to be his shadow. Guy could see that Reggie knew the restaurant better than anyone. He moved as if everything was completely second nature. He was polite with the customers, demanding with the dishwashers, and knew how to stay clear of the manager.

Guy spent the morning clearing tables and lugging dishes to the dishwashing station. If someone dropped a fork, he brought them a new one.

When breakfast service died down, Sam came in and took a booth in the restaurant by himself. Guy motioned to the section's waiter that he would get coffee for Sam. He poured a cup and added milk. He served it to Sam and nodded politely.

"How did you know to put milk in my coffee?"

"Just a guess, sir."

Sam took a sip. He pulled the napkin off the table and spread it on his lap. "This is a nice place to work, I take it?"

Guy looked around. The ceilings were high, and the chandeliers reached excessively toward an expensive-looking carpet. Otherwise, he thought, the café looked ordinary. “I hope it will be, sir.”

“Sam, please. Call me Sam. No need for *sir*.”

Guy nodded. Sam took another sip of his coffee.

“Sam, I’d like to speak to you later today, if I could.”

Guy took a rag from his apron and busily wiped down the table. Sam motioned that he sit down across from him. Guy looked around for the manager, and then back at Sam. “I’ll get fired for sure.”

“Nonsense. With what I pay to live here at the Ritz, no one bothers me, or bothers people that are with me. Understood? Let us simply talk right here.”

Guy took a seat opposite Sam. He looked around and saw the café manager talking to a customer. He could hear the manager’s voice.

“I can’t sit.”

Sam drank the rest of his coffee and set the cup lightly in its matching saucer. “Then I will pay you for the coffee and we will speak later in the day, in my apartment.”

Sam handed Guy a ten-dollar note. “Consider it your first tip,” he said.

Guy kept the bill in his hand as he watched Sam wipe his mouth and politely summon his hat from the coat-check girl. Guy placed the ten-dollar note under the coffee cup and went back to the kitchen.

The alleyway door was open, and he could see Reggie and a few others relaxing in the doorway and having a cigarette. Reggie turned, motioned Guy over, and offered him a cigarette.

“Take ten minutes. Okay? Smoke, or don’t. This is your break time now.”

After Reggie disappeared back into the restaurant, Guy cut through the staff door to the lobby. He used the elevator, his soiled apron drawing a few looks from the guests. When he made it into their room, he found Althea getting dressed.

“How’s work?”

“It’s good,” he said. He stood and watched her brush her hair. “Are you going out?”

“I am,” she said. “I have something I want to do.”

Guy went into the bathroom and washed his hands. “What is it?”

"You'll say I'm silly."

Guy dried his hands and came back to her. "I won't say you're silly. Promise." He walked over and held his hand to her forehead.

"I told you already that I felt better."

Guy pulled the room key out of his pocket and handed it to her.

"You smell like breakfast food," she said. Guy looked down at his dirty apron.

"You should come down to the café and eat. Order a cup of coffee and I'll sneak you over some food."

Althea put down her brush and put on her shoes. "Now you're the silly one."

They left the room together and rode the elevator to the lobby. Althea tugged at Guy's apron string as he walked back across the lobby toward the café.

"Not funny," he said.

Althea stepped out of the hotel and onto the boardwalk, into the misty, salty air. She headed north, toward Steel Pier. She knew it was a secret to keep, to be so early in a pregnancy. When a woman wasn't far along yet, no one noticed anything different, and you didn't tell anyone at all for fear of bad luck.

A parade of children approached, almost knocking Althea over. She stepped quickly out of the way and stood with all the others, watching and clapping.

The procession, Althea thought, seemed less a parade than a moving advertisement for a children's revue. Little boys and girls did cartwheels. One youngster juggled various items—keys and wallets and lighters that he borrowed from the crowd. At the end of the line came the singers. It was quite a spectacle, and after everything else, Althea felt relieved to simply smile and revel in their youth.

When the last of the children passed, and the wave of the previously onlooking adults resumed its slow, boardwalk shuffle, Althea walked pointedly to the fortune-teller's booth.

No one was inside. Althea stepped back onto the boardwalk and looked around for the old lady, then peeked back inside the booth and saw the fortune-teller's globe and cards. She figured the fortune-teller wouldn't have strayed very far from her wares.

Althea finally spied the fortune-teller across the boardwalk. She sat alone on a bench on the ocean side. Althea crossed the boardwalk and slowly approached her. The fortune-teller smoked a brown cigarette and muttered to herself.

"Hello," Althea said. "Do you remember me?"

The fortune-teller tossed her cigarette onto the sand below. "You came back for the reading of your cards?"

Althea smiled politely. "Not today. Thank you. I wanted to ask you a question." The fortune-teller stood and nodded. "You said something was haunting me. Was it . . . was it that I'm pregnant?"

The fortune-teller looked down at Althea's stomach. "I felt a male presence. That is all I remember."

The old woman touched Althea on the shoulder and walked slowly back to her booth.

Althea put her hand on her stomach and rubbed a circle. She tried to remember the trick with the string and the wedding ring that gave proof that a woman was carrying a boy or a girl.

Setting up for lunch service proved more difficult for Guy than clearing breakfast dishes. There was a prescribed series of steps to transition between the two meals. Every preparation, every setup, from fancy napkin folds to silverware sets, had to be done in proper fashion, and no one took the time to train Guy. Occasionally, a waiter simply yelled at him, rudely, telling him he was slowing everybody down. He felt completely in the way. He knocked into people, into things. Eventually, Reggie took him to the dishwashing station and told him to work scrubbing the heavy pots and pans for the remainder of his shift.

It was hot, grueling work, and no one at the station spoke to him. He thought about his upcoming meeting with Sam as he scrubbed. A man named Farmer Joe worked at the next sink, and Guy fell into a rhythm as he mirrored his actions. The morning crept on.

Althea had only enough money for a hot dog with mustard, and she sat on a bench near Ripley's and ate it. A crowd had just dispersed, and she watched the Ripley's workers as they set up the next sideshow. They affixed a sign to a makeshift stage that looked like a roped-off playpen.

Althea finished her hot dog and moved close enough to read the sign.

Before she could make it out, a group of men, no taller than the smallest children she had seen in the revue, climbed onstage and began to wrestle. A crowd started to form immediately, and Althea felt herself propelled by the mob toward the stage. Voices called out.

"Midget wrestling! Midget wrestling!"

Althea jostled and fought to avoid becoming one of the Ripley's crowd. After she had escaped the mob, she strolled along the boardwalk, and for the next half-mile, she found herself face-to-face with various sideshows. She tried not to look, but after passing three, she felt a desire to view them, as if they were roadside car accidents.

She stopped and watched kangaroos boxing kangaroos inside a small enclosure. She was surprised to see how angry they looked—how willing to punch one another. The crowd egged them on, and she heard people bet on the one with red gloves, or blue.

Althea walked on, past the next sideshow of tigers dressed up like ballroom dancers. No matter where she tried to go to be with her thoughts, she saw sideshows: a flea circus, a man juggling weaponry, a woman breathing fire.

Althea had seen too much. She hurried to the boardwalk's ocean side, where she hugged the railing for support. Catcalls filled the air, and she turned to watch Siamese twins stroll the middle of the promenade with a sign advertising Ripley's.

Nausea overcame Althea. She wished that she had remembered to bring her thalidomide pills with her. She stumbled to a bench near Steel Pier, sat down, and faced the ocean. Waves broke in the distance, and she concentrated as best she could on their rhythm. If she could sit still and rest, she would gather the strength, she was sure, to walk home by way of the beach.

The staff finished setting the lunch service in the café, and Reggie gave Guy a quarter of an hour for break time. Guy knew he would never make it back in fifteen minutes. He cut quickly through the lobby and into the guest elevator.

Once inside their hotel room, he noticed the clock. He would miss checkout without Althea there to pack up, and he would have to pay for another night. The room rate alone was more than he'd make for his entire day of bussing tables. He felt sure of that much.

He rode the elevator as high as he could, and then called Sam's apartment. Sam answered and told Guy that a man would come down and meet him at the elevator bay.

By the time Guy stepped into Sam's apartment, his break time had long expired.

"Good to see you looking so *tired*," Sam said. "A little play on words."

Guy sat down on a settee and immediately extracted his wallet.

"If I didn't know you so well," Sam said, "I would have thought you were pulling a pistol on me. And here am I, quietly relaxing in my Jacobean chair." He crossed his legs, took off his reading glasses, and set them on the sideboard.

"This is for you. Sir." Guy held out his wallet, and Sam took it. "The money's inside."

Sam opened the wallet. The billfold was fat, the notes sealed against one another from the pressure. "This is everything I took from the glove box of the black Ford," Guy said.

Sam wedged his thumb and forefinger into the wallet and extracted the bills. "This is *all of the money*?"

"What's left."

Sam flipped through the money as if he were shuffling a deck of cards. He put the money in his pocket and handed back the wallet.

"Was that the entire nature of your request that we speak in private?"

Guy shook his head. He felt his breathing become shallow, rapid.

"I've been thinking about everything, sir. About going to Maine to work for you, like you said. And I, well, Althea and I are going to have a baby."

Sam clapped his hands together like thunder. "What great news, my boy!"

"Yes. Yes it is. Really it is."

Sam crossed to the sideboard and poured two snifters of brandy. He handed one to Guy.

"Thank you," Guy said.

They drank their brandy in silence. Guy watched as Sam swirled and sniffed at his.

"I'll be twenty-one, soon, and then in February I'll be a father." Guy's sips were clumsy, the alcohol reminding him of Max. "I'll have people to depend on me, and on my . . . decisions. And—I—I can't do things I can't explain to my family."

Sam picked up a cigar and cut the end. He did not offer one to Guy.

"I don't even know what all has happened, sir. Everything just sort of came at me in this short time, and I don't know. But I'm asking you to let me, I'm asking you . . . " Guy stood, moved to a nearby table, and set down his snifter. "I guess I'm asking you to not make me go to Maine."

Sam lit his cigar and sat back in his chair, smoking. "This is quite a thing to consider, Guy. Of course I will have to think on it. You know this is not a crèche I'm running."

Guy walked over and extended his hand. Sam did not shake it.

"Show yourself out," he said.

A man walked purposefully toward Althea. He came from the vicinity of Steel Pier and her eye caught and held on him and for a moment the reality did not strike. It was—somehow—her father.

She knew absolutely that it was him—the way he walked, his bald head, the piercing eyes. It made no sense. They had told no one where they were going. They had called no one. It was, she thought, simply impossible.

Althea flagged down a rolling chair and got in. The operator pushed her in the direction of the Ritz. She thought about telling him to go faster, but she was sure she had simply seen a ghost. Althea placed her hand on her stomach. The nausea was not palpable anymore, but seeing her father had caused immediate, acidic distress.

The chair stopped. Her father got in, and the operator struggled with the added weight. Althea slid away from her father and placed her hands on the crossbar.

"I know you saw me coming," he said.

Althea did not look at him. She remembered reading, when she was little, that a ghost will simply disappear if a living person does not acknowledge its presence.

"You had to know I'd find you."

Althea moved to get up. Her father extended his arm and firmly gripped the crossbar on her side.

"No, no. I didn't call motels day after day and drive *all the way up here* to chase you any further."

Althea turned and looked into his eyes. She knew she had been mistaken. He would not simply vanish into thin air.

"Have to admit, Al, I almost didn't call the Ritz-Carlton. The operator said do I want to try that one, and I said, "*That's not likely*." And then I thought, well, maybe you did have some of your own money squirreled away somewhere." He pulled his hand off the bar and placed it on her knee. "Where's that *Guy* friend of yours, anyhow?"

"*Guy* is my husband now."

Her father scoffed, deep in his throat. It was a noise she remembered. "That a *fact*?"

Althea scanned the shops and faces as the chair rolled slowly along the boardwalk.

"He's not right for you, and you know that."

"*You* know that."

"I do. Hell, I *do* know that. Shame you don't, Al."

There had to be a policeman somewhere, she thought. She turned away from her father as much as she could—and there, leaning against the entrance to her booth, was the old fortune-teller. Althea thought to scream.

"Stop the chair," her father said.

The chair stopped; he reached into his pocket, and handed the operator a ten. He exited the chair, reached into Althea's lap, and tightly grasped her wrist. He pulled her down a ramp, and Althea caught a glimpse of the old fortune-teller watching them.

"My car," he said.

Althea pulled back and stopped them from walking.

"You're not taking me home," she said.

"Okay. You drive," he said. "We'll just talk."

He tossed her the keys. Althea did not catch them. She watched the sweat roll across her father's bald head. It was obvious that he had been out walking in the hot sun for some time as he tried to find her.

Her father sat down on a curb. "You're my only child, and you leave in the middle of the night and now you're married and I can't even talk to my one and only family member?"

It struck Althea that he said "my *one and only* family." Here she was, pregnant with his grandchild, and it was the one thing she knew she should not, could not tell him.

"I'll take a drive with you," she said. "But that's it."

When Guy returned to the café he realized, from the sheer size of the lunch crowd, that he was very, very late. He made his entrance quietly and hurriedly walked to the steward's area to wash dishes. Farmer Joe was not at the station, so when Guy heard footsteps approach, he assumed it was Joe.

Guy turned and saw his café manager, flanked by a man in a three-piece suit. The man in the suit bore a gold Ritz name tag that Guy couldn't quite read.

"Follow me," the man said.

The café manager shook his head as Guy started past him.

"What is it?" Guy asked. Neither man answered.

The café manager kept shaking his head, and Guy walked off with the man in the suit. They went through an unmarked kitchen door and proceeded through a catacomb of hallways. Guy finally thought to turn and run, but he wasn't sure he knew his way back.

They passed through a ballroom and entered and ascended a stairway. At its apex, the man unlocked a door marked *Private*. The door opened into an expansive office. They had entered through a back door, and the man in the suit led Guy around a far-too-large desk in the middle of the room to sit opposite himself.

"Do you know *who I am*?"

Guy shook his head.

"You shouldn't. People like you work their whole lives here at the Ritz and never know who I am. It's unfortunate for you that I know who *you* are."

"Sir?"

The man in the suit put his feet up on the desk. Guy noticed that they were oddly small.

"You're out, boy. How dare you enter *my lobby* in a shit-slop apron, and ride my damned elevator!"

Guy snorted and leaned forward to read the man's name tag.

"Don't act like you're something, *boy*. I've got half a dozen employees who have ratted you out. To think you were in *my* damned lobby!"

Guy leaned back. "My god, you're the manager of the whole hotel and this is what you do with your time? Frederick?"

"You're shit-canned, you little shit. And you're also out of my hotel room. Your bags will be at the desk. Now move the hell out!"

Guy pushed back from the desk and caught his foot on his chair as he stood. The chair toppled. He started to pick it up, but kicked it instead. He left the office without looking back.

It took him a few wrong turns to find his way through the halls. He saw a fire exit in a ballroom and took it. He was surprised to find himself immediately outside. The midday sun was striking on Guy's face, and he closed his eyes and took in its warmth. He remembered Althea saying she was going somewhere he would think silly. It came to him quickly: The fortune-teller. He felt angry at her for continuing to believe in such things.

He walked in a hurry, then ran for several minutes before realizing the tug of his apron. He took it off and threw it into a trash can. He walked on, passing restaurants and hotels, and thought about where he might work. The Blenheim was as large as the Ritz. He could get another job bussing tables.

The fortune-teller was standing outside her booth. He almost ran into her before he recognized her. She wasn't wearing a head cover, and looked no different than the woman running the fruit juice stand a few stalls over.

"Did my wife come by?" he asked.

"She rolled by in a chair," she said. "Got out of it and walked off with some man." Guy watched her pull a brown cigarette out and light it.

"A man?"

The fortune-teller ignored Guy, and smoked her cigarette.

"What did the man look like? About my age?" Guy looked up and down in each direction. "He was here on the boardwalk?"

"You okay, young man?"

"Describe him to me."

The old fortune-teller stubbed out her cigarette and put the unsmoked half back in her case. "Bald guy. Maybe fifty or so."

Guy shook his head and muttered, "*Monroe.*" He put his hand on the woman's shoulder to say thanks, then started running.

The fortune teller called out. "Wrong way!"

Guy stopped and reversed direction. He zigzagged through people without thinking, nearly overturning a stroller. He kept asking himself how Monroe could have found them. Had Althea finally given in and called?

Althea had never, ever driven her father's Mercedes. She didn't care to change that at the moment, and when they got to the car, she hesitated to place the key in the ignition.

"I'm hungry," she said. "Why don't we just walk along the boardwalk and get something to eat?"

The thought of eating a meal with her father crystallized. Images of food brought her nausea on suddenly, and she eased back in the driver's seat.

"Drive on," he said. "We'll find a place to eat something on the road."

She inhaled deeply and placed the key on the dash. "On the boardwalk in Wildwood, they have this place called 'The Nut Hut.'"

Her father put his hand softly across the back of her head.

"So, Al. We were off in Wildwood too, were we? Some honeymoon tour you're on." He tousled her hair. "If you're going to drive, Al, drive. Otherwise, let's switch seats."

Althea started the Mercedes. She put it in gear, pulled out of the parking lot, and made a right at the first intersection. She drove aimlessly, in silence. Out of the corner of her eye, she could see her father staring at her.

"This Atlantic City isn't *home*," he said.

Althea drove slowly. She looked along the skyline, searching for the Ritz.

"These northern cities and their cockeyed ideas. *Kennedy ideas.*"

"You just hate anyone different than you, Daddy. You know?"

Her father raised his arm and slapped her face. Althea's hands jerked on the wheel, and the Mercedes swerved to the right before she steadied it.

"Don't go getting all Catholic on me, young lady. You might as well have married yourself a nigger."

Althea stopped the Mercedes in the middle of the street. A horn honked, and then a car went around them.

"Why did you come here? To remind me why I left?"

Her father took a deep breath and exhaled. "You can't spend the rest of your life with this Pope of yours."

Althea turned off the Mercedes. She reached for the handle of her door.

"No, Al. I'm sorry." He motioned for her to restart the car. "Let's just drive a little bit more. I promise I'll hear your side in this."

Althea started the Mercedes and drove on. She had no idea where she was going.

"There's nothing to say, Daddy. Guy and I are married now. He's my husband and we're—"

"What? You're what? *Happy?*"

Althea nodded.

"That's it exactly," she said. "We're happy."

Guy slowed his pace. He calmed himself reasoning that if Althea and Monroe had been in a rolling chair together, things must be going okay. Maybe, he thought, her father had just wanted to come up and see her. Maybe she had called him and he had brought her some of her money after all.

His throat dried up. He had to slow to a walk. They were probably heading, he thought, to the Ritz. Maybe they were hoping to visit him at the café. He felt somehow sure of it. His pace quickened when he caught sight of the Ritz.

Once inside the hotel, Guy made his way carefully through the lobby. He knew he had to avoid being seen, or he might be thrown out onto the promenade, along with his bags. The café had emptied out, and Guy managed to view the entire seating area before any staff member saw him.

The elevator was free, and he rode it to his floor and went to his room. The door was wide open, the radio was on, and a maid was bent over, cleaning up the dried blood in the bathroom. Otherwise, the room contained no visible trace of him and Althea ever having slept there.

Guy went back to the elevator bay, pushed the button, and waited. Maybe, he thought, her father had no interest in a peaceful visit. Guy started picturing exactly how things went between Althea and her father. He thought of the time she locked herself in her room and he had come at the door with a ten-pound hammer.

The elevator whirred, and the door opened. He stepped in and rode it back down to the first floor.

In the crowded lobby, Sam passed him. For a moment, Guy's eyes followed Sam. And then the idea hit.

He managed to turn and weave through the crowd and grabbed Sam just as they reached the main doors to the boardwalk.

"I need you," Guy said.

Sam took up a seat on the velvet couch, and Guy joined him.

"You look like a ghost," Sam said. "Alright, tell me what it is."

"Althea," Guy said. "I think her father came up here to take her back home."

Sam folded the newspaper he carried and tapped it on his knee. "I see. Her father—he is the kind of man that would take Althea against her wishes?"

Guy's clenched fists had begun to hurt. He stretched out his fingers and twisted his wedding ring. "He is, Sam. And I'm sure he's here. He hates it more than anything that she's with me."

Sam laughed quietly. "But surely he must see that you two are adults? Yes?"

Guy shook his head. "No, Sam. Her father swore to her he wouldn't let her marry a Catholic. It's the main reason we eloped. I know it's why he's here."

Sam sat back, lifted his head, and looked up at the high ceiling. "What is the gentlemen's name?"

"Monroe," Guy said. "He was a Grand Dragon or something. Whatever they call it."

"A Klansman? Lord, Lord, yes, I'm familiar with their *ornery* way of thinking."

Guy moved in closer to Sam. "They had the Klan up here?"

Sam laughed. This time it was loud, and purposeful.

"The Klan was *everywhere* when I was young, my friend. Must have been five million of them during prohibition."

Guy stood up. "Then you know how they get. You have to help me find her, Sam."

Sam stood, and squeezed Guy's shoulder.

"Stay here. Keep your eye out for them. I will be back in a few minutes."

Guy watched Sam disappear into the crowd near the elevator. Then he walked over to the café. Reggie and the others were taking down the lunch service. There was no sign of Althea or Monroe.

Sam appeared with the large man Guy had met, and the three of them exited into the parking lot. Guy and Sam got into the back of Sam's black Imperial. The large man closed their doors and took his place behind the wheel.

"When my driver gets us to the Five Hundred Club, Guy, you don't talk unless you are asked a question. Understood?"

Guy nodded. They drove for a few minutes in silence.

"You will follow me into the club, but you will sit at a table by yourself while I speak with some acquaintances of mine." Sam took a bottle of Scotch off the rack and held it aloft.

"A drink, to *steel* your nerves?"

"No, sir."

Sam placed the bottle back in its holder. "What kind of car does Monroe drive? Or do you think he came here by other means?"

"No, I'm sure that he drove. He's in love with his Mercedes."

"Virginia plates?"

Guy nodded.

Sam's driver stopped the Imperial and opened the doors. Guy followed a few steps behind the two men.

Inside the Five Hundred Club, Sam's driver ushered Guy to a table near the bar, then accompanied Sam into a private back room. A waiter brought Guy a house drink, and Guy sat and stirred it with the swizzle stick. The club was dark, even during daylight hours. A deep smell of alcohol pervaded the room, and though the walls displayed pictures of famous entertainers, Guy realized the Five Hundred Club represented the kind of decay Sam had been talking about. No one seemed to care about all the dirt and grime, and Guy could feel his shoes sticking to the carpet. It seemed as though sunlight had never found its way into the club.

Guy was sitting too far from the private room to make out the conversation, but the name "Monroe Gearheart" was audible. He thought he heard an older man say the word "Klansman" slowly, and in an obvious, harsh tone.

The waiter had twice checked on Guy before Sam came out of the private room and joined Guy at his table. Sam grabbed the house drink and swallowed the concoction in one gulp.

"Cigar, Guy?"

Guy shook his head. Sam cut and lit his cigar and puffed on it repeatedly.

"I am positive we will locate them rather quickly," he said. "I have called in several favors on your behalf."

Guy dropped his head and rubbed his knuckles into his crew-cut. A few men spilled out of the back room, and one of them slapped Guy hard across the back. Guy turned and watched him walk out the front door.

"That man in the fedora, Sam; when he slapped me on the back, it reminded me of Max."

"Ah, yes. Max. The elephant in the room." Sam jammed out his cigar in the ashtray. "You know, Max was about your age, maybe a little younger, when I first encountered him. He was up here in Atlantic City with his girl, Jeannie. Played a bit of cards at the time, young Max."

Another man came out of the back room. He took a seat in a chair that blocked the door to the private entrance.

"I didn't mean to mention Max," Guy said. "Sorry."

Sam waved him off and smiled. "I rescued Max. He had gotten in over his head at a card game he should not have attended. I knew the man he owed. I paid the debt down, and Max went to work for me. Set him up in the Wildwoods."

"I see," Guy said.

Sam folded his arms across his chest. "But he got in with the wrong people down there. Took on a job he should not have taken."

The front door opened again, and Guy anxiously peered out, looking for the Imperial. He started to ask Sam to drive him around to look for Althea.

"Guy. Have patience. We are in good hands. Even if they are a hundred miles away, we will find them, and Althea will be brought right here."

Guy fidgeted with the empty glass on the table.

"Monroe drives a Mercedes, then. Is it a Gullwing?" Sam asked.

Guy shrugged and slid the glass around in the pool of water it had made.

"If it was a Gullwing Mercedes, you would know it. No matter. I'm just a curious sort."

Althea was done with driving around in circles. She needed, she knew, to simply get out of the car, and away from her father. Everything he had said and done had offended her, and she knew that he had no plan beyond simple intimidation. At least he had finally stopped talking.

The silence of the car ride lulled Althea, and it took her a moment to comprehend the flashing lights in her rearview mirror.

"Cops," Monroe said.

One of the police cars pulled in front of Althea and stopped her. The other pulled alongside. An officer exited from the passenger side of the police car next to her, and Monroe got out of the car. She could not hear what the officer said to him. She watched the officer place his hand on his hip.

A scuffing noise came from behind her. In the side view mirror, she saw an officer running. He disappeared from sight, and she turned and watched through the front windshield as the two officers paired and violently collided with Monroe. The three men tangled on the grassy berm, and Althea firmly gripped the wheel and winced as they handcuffed her father.

"Everything is okay," a voice said.

Althea heard the words, but could not attach them to anyone. The voice spoke again, and she heard what sounded like a ring tapping her window. She stared at her father as an officer in her periphery motioned for her to turn off the Mercedes. Althea un-gripped the steering wheel.

The police car in front of her pulled away, and she watched the back of her father's head grow small in the distance. The remaining officer opened her door.

"Are you okay to drive, then? Can you follow us?"

"What's going on?"

"Your father is under arrest. An outstanding warrant, I think."

Althea slammed her hands onto the steering wheel. In her mind she tried to connect the word "outstanding" to her father.

"Young lady, can you drive?"

Althea nodded.

"It isn't far," the officer said. "Just follow me. Calmly. Okay?"

Althea watched the officer get back in his car and drive. She followed closely behind.

"Calm down, Al, calm down," she said.

She could no longer see the police car that took away her father. The streets were largely unfamiliar to her, and she could not find any landmarks she knew.

The police car she was following pulled into a parking lot behind a building. Althea looked around for the precinct. She did not see it. The police car stopped, and the officer got out and walked toward her.

"Okay," he said. "Come on with me."

He motioned with his hands for Althea. She turned off the Mercedes and got out. He led the way to the building's back door and opened it for her.

They walked through a hallway and entered a large room. It was somewhat dark inside.

Sam spotted her first. He waved his arms and the officer pointed her in his direction. Guy stood and crossed the room to meet Althea. They embraced.

"My father was arrested," she said.

Guy led her to their table, and Sam pulled out a chair. "Please, sit," Sam said.

Althea looked at Guy, then at Sam.

"I believe we all know one another?" Sam asked.

Althea nodded at him. He smiled at her. Guy took her hand in his.

"Sam lives at the Ritz. I asked him to help me find you."

Althea stared at Sam as Guy spoke. "The fortune-teller told me she saw you," Guy said. "I figured it out from there."

Althea turned and looked around the room. The movement exposed her cheek.

"He hit you, *again*," Guy said.

Althea's hand went to her face.

"Where are we?" she asked.

"The Five Hundred Club," Sam said. Guy moved closer and studied Althea's face.

"Bastard," he said.

"Your father," Sam said. "I understand he is far from a good man."

Althea pushed her chair away from the table. She kept touching her cheek lightly with her fingertips. "It's nothing," she said. "I'm okay."

"Perhaps I tell you a story, Althea. To take your mind elsewhere. Yes? That seat you are in, right where you are now. I had lunch while Frank Sinatra sat right there. He sat *exactly* where you are sitting now."

"Where is my father?"

Sam laughed. "I imagine, not where he would like to be?"

"He's in jail?"

Sam laughed again. "In a way, yes. He's being, let us say, *spoken to*."

Guy scooted his chair closer to Althea's.

"About what? His warrant?" she asked.

Sam leaned toward her. "There is no warrant, Althea. That is all part of the ruse we play with the police. A kind of two-step, if you will. Your father is being persuaded to leave you alone. Which, as I gathered from Guy, is the problem at hand. And I gather it even more, now, having heard that he has struck you, historically."

"Don't hurt him," Althea said. "There's no reason to, really. Please." She said it with a break in her voice.

"I am not going to lay a finger on him, my dear."

Guy looked from Althea to Sam.

"No one will hurt your father," Sam said. "You have my word that he is simply being dissuaded from contacting you again in person. Until you tell me to tell them otherwise, of course."

Althea lowered her head into her hands. Sam nodded at Guy and continued.

"You know, the three of us are much alike, from what information I have. I myself was an orphan, a ward of the state. I was taken in by a Jewish woman, who had lived alone, when I was just a boy. She schooled me and raised me and became my mother. The only family I ever knew."

"Sounds like an angel," Guy said.

"She was."

Sam's driver came over, and he and Sam stepped away from the table to talk. Althea and Guy sat in silence for a minute. Then Guy spoke.

"I've decided, after everything that's happened, that I want to have the baby baptized. Okay? Two weeks after it's due, I think, is Ash Wednesday. Can we do that?"

"I want to leave," Althea said.

Guy stood up and pulled out her chair. Sam's driver came over and blocked their way.

"I am to drive you to your destination," he said.

He led them outside and helped Althea into the backseat of the Imperial. Guy got in next to her.

"Where's Sam? " Guy asked.

Sam's driver started the engine and drove out of the parking lot. "He had other business."

Althea and Guy sat in the spacious Imperial and stared out the little triangle window that flanked the vast backseat.

It was a short ride to the Ritz to collect their bags. Sam's driver retrieved them and deposited them in the trunk. He got back in the car and drove out of town onto a main highway. Althea asked Guy where they were going in a whisper. Guy did not know, and he did not answer.

Outside, it was still a bit more day than night. Inside the Imperial, Althea felt sleepy, as if it were closer to midnight. She leaned across the seat and rested her head on Guy. He brushed aside the hair that hid her bruised cheek.

"It's okay," he said.

The scenery sped past. The immense size of the Imperial created an illusion. Outside, it appeared as if the world was hurtling by—inside, it appeared as if they were on a long, leisurely, country drive.

Atlantic City's environs gave way to intermittent watersheds and marshlands. They were heading north—that much they knew. Althea's breathing slowed, and Guy tried not to move a muscle as she slept against him. The Imperial's leather seats were well crafted, supportive, but the slightest movements produced buzzing vibrations.

The miles rolled on and Guy felt his own breathing flatten out. He knew whatever came next would be somehow better than what had come before. He pictured their leaving Atlantic City as an exodus from Althea's father. His thoughts became wildly positive images of his soon-to-be prodigy: Althea nursing the newborn; his uncle, as godfather, christening the baby; the child holding a fresh-picked apple from the family farm. Soon Guy entered a relaxed, deep slumber.

The blare of a train horn in the distance woke Guy. Althea's hair was across his mouth and he brushed it away and breathed deeply. Through the Imperial's triangular window, he saw the larger road dwindle into a smaller one.

The Imperial turned onto an unpaved road. The large vehicle shimmied as it struggled to transverse the ruts and large, loose rocks.

Althea woke. She pulled herself back to her side of the Imperial and looked outside. "Where are we?"

Sam's driver muttered to himself as the Imperial lodged itself in a rut. "Well, I think that's as far as I can take you."

Althea and Guy looked at one another.

"We're getting out for good?" Guy asked. "Here?"

"I'd say so. I'll need a hand to push it."

Guy got out, and Althea followed him. Sam's driver had walked to the front hood. He placed his hands on the Imperial and pushed. Guy joined him, and together, they rocked and rolled the Imperial back and forth, again and again.

"Young lady," Sam's driver said, "get in, please, and be sure to make sure that it's in neutral."

Althea got behind the wheel. "If we get going," Sam's driver said, "just steer and brake."

Althea nodded and adjusted the mirror. They continued rocking the Imperial and got it moving. The loose rocks gave, and Althea turned the wheel and let the Imperial roll until it was completely out of the rut. The men stopped following the car, and she applied the brake, put the Imperial in park, and got out.

Sam's driver turned and pointed toward a hedgerow atop a small hill.

"This is what Sam said to tell you," he said. "I think I have it memorized."

Althea joined Guy, and he took her hand.

"'Althea and Guy. This house is my wedding present to you. It was my mother's house before she passed away a few months ago. I hope you spend many years here together raising your family.' "

Sam's driver tipped his hat at the couple. Althea placed her hand on her stomach and smiled. "Oh my God," she said.

Althea walked over and kissed Sam's driver on the cheek. She turned and smiled at Guy, then hurried up the hill toward the tall row of hedges. Guy followed. They came together at the break of the small hill, and stood and stared at the wraparound porch of the quaint bungalow.

"It's beautiful," Althea said. "I can hear—I can smell the ocean!"

Behind them, Guy heard a car door close. He turned and saw Sam's driver extracting their bags from the trunk of the Imperial. Guy met him halfway. Sam's driver smiled.

"Congratulations to both of you," he said.

Guy took the bags from him, set them down, and the two shook hands. Sam's driver gave a final wave and Guy watched the Imperial slowly depart. When Guy finally turned around, he saw that Althea had walked most of the way to the bungalow's wraparound porch. He smiled and ran after her.

He caught her at the threshold and picked her up. They kissed, and he carried her inside. Althea laughed.

"I guess we're married now," she said. "The honeymoon's over."

Guy placed Althea down on a couch. The bungalow was a bit dark inside, and Guy pushed at a couple bronze buttons for the lights.

"No electricity," he said.

"It's been empty," Althea said. "Smells stale."

Guy went over to the living room and forced opened a window.

"Yes. Open them all," Althea said. She stood and walked across the small living room, then took a seat on an old yellow chair and looked around.

"It's nice enough," she said. "It's like a cabin. You have to get it ready for the season."

Guy finished opening all the windows in the living room and the one bedroom. He stood back and took it in.

"It's big enough for three," he said. "The baby can sleep with us."

He left Althea sitting there and walked outside and down the hill for the bags. He turned and looked back at the bungalow as he walked.

As he approached the bags, his attention turned to a little space where the zipper had opened on one of the duffels. A corner of paper protruded, and he unzipped the bag and pulled out a folded envelope.

The note was from Sam. Guy read it aloud.

"Guy. This house will be yours, of course, only on the condition that we stay in business together. Harvey Cedars, New Jersey, is the perfect spot for Althea to make a home for you and your baby while you are exploring our business opportunities in Maine. I took possession of Max's Hawk, as Jeannie does not drive. It is yours to use in your travels. You will find a thousand dollars with this note and more will be sent, along with the deed to the house and the title to, and delivery of the Hawk. Again, all of this is contingent on the decision you make. I will be in contact soon. Sam."

Guy exhaled. He stuffed the note, envelope, and the thousand dollars into his pants pocket, then slid Max's jacket out of the duffel. He put the jacket on and turned. He could see, in the distance, a path that led away from the bungalow, and he took it. The path led through a bramble of honeysuckle and into a clearing, then stopped on the bay side of the narrow strip of land on which their new house rested.

It was the gloaming, but he could still make out a lone seagull strolling a rocky patch on the nearby bank. Guy turned and looked at the bungalow. The sun glinted peacefully off the apex of the tin roof, and he could see the outline of apple trees in the far side of the yard.

Guy turned and walked back. He wanted to help Althea unpack their belongings. He knew he could come back amid the bleak of midnight, to the bay, and he could hold Althea's hand and together they could watch the moon rise over and envelop the house.

About the Author

Photo by Kelly M. Zuras

Richard Lee Zuras was born and raised in Arlington, Virginia. He spent time with his parents and brother, most every summer, in Wildwood, New Jersey, and Atlantic City, New Jersey. It is from these experiences, and his vivid, undying memories of the Jersey Shore that Richard produced *The Honeymoon Corruption*. Richard now resides in northern Maine where he teaches creative writing and film at the University of Maine at Presque Isle. He lives with his wife, Kelly, and their two boys, Everett and Holden. Richard has published short stories in close to twenty literary journals and is the author of the novel *The Bastard Year* (Brandylane).

www.ingramcontent.com/pod-product-compliance
Lightning Source LLC
Chambersburg PA
CBHW051306250626
47155CB00009B/3453

* 9 7 8 1 9 3 9 9 3 0 3 9 2 *